Adriana's Eyes and Other Stories

For Stella and Seamus,
because you've been so good
to us —

All the best,

Anthony

8-30-00

Also By Anthony Maulucci

The Discovery of Luminous Being, a novel

Adriana's Eyes
and Other Stories ⚜

Anthony Maulucci

Lorenzo Press

Some of the stories in this collection originally appeared in the following publications: *Gone, The Red Fox Review*, and *Connecticut Artists*.

Typeset by Swordsmith Productions

FIRST EDITION, First Printing

Library of Congress Card Number: 98-75406
ISBN 0-9645-2261-6

The author wishes to thank the following individuals for their friendship and support: David Alvarez, Don Gastwirth, Anne Greene, Sally Maulucci, Herb Gerjuoy, James Coleman, Thomas Palmer, Mary Auslander, Robert Giroux, William Stull, Peter McClure and Elissa Fitzgerald.

For Janet, naturally

Contents &

The Madman of Long Island ⚜

DAVE GORDON WALKED into Joe Allen's bar relieved to be in out of the afternoon rain. The crowd was sparse but congenial. Most of the people seemed to know each other and be on common territory. Dave Gordon saddled himself onto a bar stool, ordered a Dewar's on the rocks and immediately started to relax. This wasn't his usual watering hole, and he felt comfortable about not seeing anyone he knew. His wife was used to this buffer time between the office and home: No phone call was necessary.

Dave Gordon finished his first drink and motioned to the bartender for another. He studied himself in the mirror while waiting. His brown hair was thinning on top but there were no lines in his face and no other signs that he was approaching thirty-one. He was still handsome and youthful. He could start over again if necessary. He told himself he had nothing to worry about on that score. But inside he felt anxiety and the strain of a busy day melding into an alloy of pain he did not understand.

Although he had grown up in Connecticut, Gordon called

1

New York City his home and believed that it was only there that he could live out his full potential as a writer and a man. He recalled the advice an early Manhattan friend had given him: "The first day you lose your job, the second day you're on the streets, and the third day you're on a train back to hicksville." According to the friend, a veteran New Yorker, that was what happened to you when you were washed up in the Big Apple. She even went so far as to suggest that this was New York's way of dealing with losers. Gordon knew he wasn't a loser, but he wasn't quite a winner yet, either. Then he laughed out loud at himself and heard the silence stretch out around him. David Gordon was laughing at himself because he had just been fired. His laughter had no pleasure in it and no pain, it was just a simple physical imperative. It was his second such imperative of the day: The first had erupted in his editor's office in the building that housed the world's most influential newspaper. Up until then, Gordon hadn't even been aware that writers were fired from The New York Times. That first laugh had cost him his future as a newspaper reporter, Gordon knew. But he didn't care. It also saved his sanity.

Every time the alarm rang, it drove a sharp nail of pain and irritation into the coffin of sleep. Finally, the coffin was sealed tight. Dave Gordon was wide awake and instantly confronted by the specter of an empty day. But routine would carry him past the morning. His wife was awake and looking at him. Without time to consider whether or not he should inform her of his new status as ex-Times man, Gordon's automatic reflexes took over. He scrambled out of bed and launched into his morning exercises, stretching his tall, lean body, pushing himself farther than usual to camouflage the sting of cowardice and confusion with strenuous exertion. Rita Gordon, dark-haired and dusky like her husband, unaware of anything out of the ordinary, got up and padded naked down the hallway into the bathroom.

By the time Gordon had showered, shaved, and dressed, he knew that his breakfast would be ready. He walked into the kitchen and sat down at the table. This was his crucible. Should he come right out and tell his wife that he had been fired or should he pretend that everything was going along normally, as it had for the last two years? Gordon forked up his scrambled eggs and chomped down on a corner of wheat toast. His wife was drinking her coffee. Her early summer tan was fading into the tawny color of her bathrobe. She poured his tea, added honey, and placed the cup by his left hand.

"Are you working in the office today, or on assignment?" Rita said.

Gordon looked up suspiciously, but everything was as normal. He had only the time it takes to swallow to make up his mind. "I'll be out of the office all day," he replied vaguely. "What about you?"

"I'll be in the studio all day with that new client."

"Sounds like a strain."

"He's a sweet man but he's always coming on to me. He thinks every woman secretly wants to go to bed with him."

"I know the type. I suppose it's part of your job to keep him interested."

"A little flirtation is good for business. It's only a problem when it interferes with my work, but I never allow it to get out of hand."

"I guess that' s the professional in you."

"We're a little testy this morning, aren't we?"

"Sorry. It's just the thought of these sleazy types undressing you with their little pig-eyes."

"Hey, do you think I enjoy it? I'm not responsible for what

goes on in their dirty little minds. Every business has its sordid side. Fashion photography is slightly more sordid than others."

"Some days I feel like buying a machine gun, that's all."

"You knew what I had to put up with when you married me."

"That doesn't make it any easier to deal with."

"What's eating you this morning anyway?"

"I don't know. I guess I'm just worried about this assignment."

"You're the best damn feature writer the Times has ever had, what have you got to worry about?"

"I don't know. Nothing, I guess."

Dave Gordon left his apartment on the Upper West Side and walked down Sixty-fourth Street to Central Park. The June morning was unseasonably cool and balmy. Gordon felt uneasy with himself as he kept pace with the commuter crowds rushing off to work, but he didn't identify his uneasy feeling until he was walking alone along a path through the Park: It was anger. Anger with an intensity he had never experienced before. He had only been joking when he told Rita that some days he felt like going out and buying a machine gun, but now he seemed close to translating that impulse into action. In the cinema of his mind, he watched himself purchase the weapon and track down his first victims: The female editor who had fired him without explanation, just the usual bullshit about his attitude being bad because he was too good to be a newspaper reporter and he knew it. He watched as if he were a movie camera, with only the barrel of the gun protruding into view as he walked down the aisle through the office, past the familiar faces frozen in horror, to the desk where she sat typing and then turned around to catch the full frontal attack of the hungry metal bullets.

Then Gordon's outburst of anger melted down into guilt. His

Catholic upbringing had provided him with a lifetime supply of fissionable guilt. A guilt which robbed him of his vitality and spontaneity, the great debilitizer of his life force and at the same time the goad of his will to work, to make something of himself.

He had walked to the bandshell and sat down on a bench in the sun to observe the activity there. Already this area of the park was thronged with winos, leftover hippies, rollerbladers and throwers of ubiquitous Frisbees. It was like looking into a human sewer, Gordon thought. He watched them with disdain. This is the Pepsi generation, he thought, the children of the universe. This is what's become of the lilies of the field. Look at them, they probably haven't got two original ideas to rub together. All they think about is how to amuse themselves, and all they do is fuck each other in packs. They live absolutely useless lives. I went through a brief stage like that back in the 'sixties, but at least I grew out of it. I guess they've spent too many hours in front of the lobotomy tube. And yet they seem happy. It doesn't make any sense, how could they be happy living useless lives?

Gordon left the Park and walked down Fifth Avenue. Fifth Avenue cheered him up. He always garnered a good feeling from looking at the beautiful things men and women created for their pleasure and amusement. Following up on this sensation, he went into the Museum of Modern Art to see Picasso's Damoiselle d'Avignon and was there until late afternoon. After lunch, he went into the library to read.

Rita was not home when he arrived at his usual time, so he fixed himself a scotch and settled down to read the book he'd taken home from the library. Strangely, he read in a self-satisfied sense of accomplishment: An entire day of non-productivity had passed without causing him to become depressed or despondent. And stranger still, the thought of looking for another job had never once crossed his mind. He was reading the biography of a man who fought against all odds to make himself a novelist. Gordon's pulse quickened as he read the part about how the writer quit his job in New York, sold all his belongings, put that money with his savings, and went to Paris to live cheaply and write his first novel. Gordon became so excited that he had to stop reading. He put the book away, poured himself another drink, and lapsed into a daydream about how he too would do it.

Rita came in an hour later electrified with good news. She dropped her cameras on the sofa and let her portfolio slide to the carpet. Her face was lit up like a blast furnace.

"I got the assignment," she cried. "Quick, give me a drink."

"What assignment?" Gordon was irked by her excitement.

"The assignment from Vogue. Didn't I tell you? Is there any gin or vodka in the house? I really need a drink, I had to walk twenty blocks."

They went into the large kitchen, the warmest room in the apartment, where their cat slept perpetually on the window ledge, and Gordon poured his wife a screwdriver.

"What assignment from Vogue?"

"I really didn't tell you? I've been so damn busy lately. Ah, that tastes good. Can you believe it, Vogue magazine is sending me to Rome!"

"For how long and for what?"

"For three weeks to shoot a new designer's line. I've got to leave tomorrow, and I've got a million things to do. Aren't you happy for me, darling?"

"I think it's great. What a coincidence."

"A coincidence? What do you mean?"

"The Times is sending me to Washington for a month to do a series on diplomats."

The lie came out automatically, and Gordon really believed it as he said it. Rita hugged him and said something about how exciting their lives were. Gordon didn't hear her. He was genuinely pleased by his sudden decision. He knew he was going away, but not to Washington.

He had enough money in his savings account to go to Paris, but Gordon decided instead to go to the summer house he and Rita had rented at Amagansett on Long Island. This time away from New York City would be his personal moratorium. He wanted to stand back at a distance, gain some perspective, and determine what the next major step of his life would have to be.

Gordon moved into the three-bedroom house with a suitcase and a typewriter and a few bottles of scotch. He promised himself he would stay there until he had written three good chapters of a novel. He knew he needed to prove to himself that he could do it.

Shaped like the capital letter H, the kitchen and living room forming the crossbar and the bedrooms making up the vertical lines, the house was situated on a hill overlooking the sea. Living there without Rita, sleeping alone, eating alone, and spending the evenings alone, was disorienting. Gordon had plenty of time to wonder why he hadn't told her he'd been fired. Why had he kept up the pretense that he still had a job and everything was fine? Pride seemed so silly now. Rita would have understood. Now she was in Rome, and she was probably too busy to miss him. Why hadn't he gone with her? Everything had happened so damn fast. This was the first time they'd been apart since they were married, and Gordon was feeling lost and lonely. Work would have to sustain him. But what if he couldn't start his novel, couldn't get his bearings? Would he commit some desperate act? Long Island was the perfect place for it, he chuckled grimly to himself, a limbo between Connecticut and New York. And maybe suicide would be the perfect solution to a life of misused talent. Death would be the end of all his pain, too. Why was he cursed with the desire to be a great artist? What would it matter if he never wrote his great novel, his magnum opus? And if he did manage to write it the way he wanted to, would the world be any better for it? Why did he let such things worry him so much? He was overly sensitive, as Rita had once said, he had an over-refined sensibility. He was ashamed of his effete sensitivity. It was unmanly. But that's what comes of being in the city too long and living on nervous energy, he thought, and that's what comes of associating with neurotic writers and artists who go around with their entrails exposed and quivering to every stimulus that comes along. That's why I drink so much, Gordon mused, not to heighten my senses but to deaden them. I allow myself to feel too damn much, just like Van Gogh. He must have killed himself because the intensity of his feelings was too painful to bear.

For days, Gordon contemplated a romantic death and imagined himself becoming a part of the honorable tradition established by Shelley, Van Gogh, and Hemingway. In that frame of mind, he began writing his novel. Hope and a sense of destiny did not sustain him as much as sheer desperation, which gave him the momentum to follow through on his creative impulse. By the end of the first week, a routine was entrenched in his new, good life: He awoke at dawn, bicycled to the beach, had a swim, bicycled back to the house, took a shower, had breakfast and started writing. He spent the afternoons running errands and the evenings writing and reading.

Gordon wrote in a room at the end of the house which commanded an unobstructed view of the ocean. One morning while he was working, his cat curled up on his feet, Gordon saw what he thought was a barrel bobbing up and down in the waves about a hundred feet from the shore. The sight of the object reminded him of a man's head, and he studied it until he was struck with a brilliantly vivid image that immediately became part of the paragraph he was at work on. The writing was going well. When he looked up from the paper again, staring automatically out at the ocean, Gordon's eyes searched for the object, found it and fixed on it. Then he jumped up in alarm and went close to the window. The object was closer now and Gordon realized with a shock that it was a person who appeared to be drowning in the sea. Instantly, he was running out of the house, leaping on his bicycle, and riding as fast as he could go down the hill to the beach. The beach was deserted and Gordon ran across it to the spot where he had last seen the bobbing head. He caught sight of it again about twenty-five feet from shore, and as he did he kicked off his sneakers, pulled off his shirt, and ran in over the waves. Gordon was not a strong swimmer, but the distance was short and the waves were small. He reached the drowning figure, which turned out to be a man, with just enough strength to pull him back to shore.

Back on land, on the sand in the sunlight, Gordon pumped the water out of the man's lungs and held his own breath while the nearly drowned man gasped for his. Then Gordon rolled him over and sat beside him, each man panting for breath and straining to catch his normal rhythm while the waves swept at regular intervals across the shore. Gordon looked at the man whose life he had saved. He appeared to be about fifty or fifty-five, and he was completely dressed in black. His nose had been broken, his cheekbones were high and prominent, his iron-gray hair was short and thick, and his beard was pointed like a pharaoh's. Gordon stared at him, wondering who he could be and what had happened to him. Then the survivor opened his eyes—they were a startling blue, like the sky—and stared back at Gordon. Neither man spoke, but neither man looked away, and in those silent seconds Gordon felt a bond of brotherhood spinning out between himself and the strange man who lay there like a small beached whale. And he thought: Maybe this man wanted to die and now he will hate me for saving his life. Suddenly the man in black smiled and said, "I tried to swim like Ulysses."

"You almost made it."

"But with almost I would be dead. I am glad you were there to complete the almost."

He ended his sentence with a cough and tried to get up. Gordon moved behind him and lifted him to his feet. He was shorter than Gordon but heavy and solidly built.

"Can you walk?" said Gordon.

"Yeah, better than I can swim."

"Let me help you. My house isn't far from here. You can rest there."

The man was very weak and leaned on Gordon for support. Slowly and without speaking they walked up the hill to the house. By the time they arrived, the man was too weak to talk. Gordon took off his wet clothes, put him into a bed, and made him a cup of hot tea. By the time he brought in the tea, the man was asleep.

Gordon sat behind his typewriter for the rest of the morning, but his curiosity about the man's identity prevented him from going on with his work. By noon the man was awake and vigorous. He came out of the bedroom looking for his clothes. Gordon heard him and came out of his study.

"Your clothes are still wet. I'll give you something to wear."

"No. I want my clothes," said the man.

They went out into the backyard. The man took his clothes

from the line, shook them out and put them on. Then he turned around to face Gordon.

"A man who is not wearing his clothes cannot look another man squarely in the eye," he said. Taking two steps forward in his bare feet, he shook Gordon's hand, looking at him steadily and with gratitude in his blue eyes.

The two men stood staring at each other. There was something haunting them: The need for something more to be said. The sound of the ocean came up from below; there were the cries of gulls riding overhead. Gordon sensed that the other man was uncomfortable, so he said, "Do you want something to eat? I was going to make myself some lunch."

"Excellent. Drowning gives a man an appetite."

Barbecuing steaks on a grill, they drank beer and talked. The man called himself Niko and said he was a sculptor who earned his living by hiring himself out as a fisherman during the mako shark season. He laughingly said he was known on the Island as Crazy Niko because he would go out on any boat in any kind of weather. He had almost drowned this morning because he had gone out on an unfit boat in unfit weather. Niko had lived on the Island for twenty years and declared he would never live anywhere else, especially not the city. He loved sculpting and fishing and swore he would never do anything else.

"Do you make enough money during the mako shark season to support yourself for the rest of the year?"

"Money. How much does a man need? Life is simple. It's people who make it complicated and expensive."

"But everybody needs money to live."

"Of course everybody needs money to live, but most people stop living when they start making money. I take only what I need."

Gordon stared with fascination at his guest. His body had

around it an aura of being alive—despite the fact that he had almost drowned. His eyes were clear, his face animated, and his movements were vigorous and spare. Niko spoke with the authority and power of a man who knew himself, who had explored his own depths with greater courage and at greater risk than was demanded of him on the sea. As he watched him, Gordon realized that he had the face of a man who knows no fear.

"I will tell you about making money," Niko exclaimed suddenly. "Do you want to know the secret of making money? It's this: You make money by exploiting people's pretensions. Whether you are a sculptor, a writer, or a salesman. The principle is the same. You make people think that by buying what you have to offer they will become what they want to be or what they think they are, and they will pay you any amount of money for the privilege."

Gordon thought about this for a moment and then said, "So what's wrong with that?"

"Nothing. There's nothing wrong with that, if that's the way you want to live your life."

"Look, poverty can be just as destructive as greed."

"I'm not talking about poverty," Niko replied calmly. "I'm talking about moderation."

The two men were silent again, each musing over his own thoughts. The warmth of the afternoon sun, the playful breeze, the sound of insects, the taste of the food and the smell of the ocean wove a special atmosphere around them, into the texture of their thoughts and words, and became a part of the pleasure they were feeling in each other's company.

But when they finished eating and were smoking cigarettes, Niko was staring at Gordon with an arch look on his suddenly mephisthophelean face. "Let me ask you a question," he said.

"Why do you let your feelings show so much? A man needs a protective shell in order to survive. How can you go through the world so completely naked?"

Gordon was taken aback. He blushed, his face burned hot, and he could not get his eyes to look Niko straight in the face. "What are you talking about?" he stammered lamely.

"I only say this to you because I like you. Exposing your feelings, you put yourself at the mercy of other people. You let other people get the better of you, and it shows a lack of courage. That's all I have to say. Now I must go. I must find out what has happened to the others."

Niko stood up. Gordon stood up with him, still blushing and unable to think of a rebuttal. All he could say was, "I'll walk you to the road."

They walked again along the road from the house but this time apart and independent. Gordon could not understand the reason for Niko's criticism. What hurt was that his feelings for the man were warm and congenial, he was ready to offer his friendship and hoped it would be reciprocated. He supposed that this was too obviously and eagerly displayed on his face and had put the other man off.

At the junction of the road which ran along the beach into town, Gordon retrieved his bicycle.

"I owe my life to you and the invention of the bicycle," Niko said, shaking Gordon's hand firmly. "If you want to talk some more, come tonight at seven to a bar called The Docksider. I'll be there then."

"I'll come."

"Until then," said Niko, walking away with a wave of his hand and the flash of a quick smile.

"Wait," Gordon called after him. "Why don't you take my bicycle, it's a long walk."

"You better keep it," Niko called back without turning around. "You never know who might be drowning this afternoon."

For the rest of the day, Gordon mulled over the events of the morning and afternoon. He pulls a drowning man out of the ocean, virtually carries him home, puts him to bed, feeds him, and then this man has the audacity to tell him he lacks courage because he lets his feelings show. What the hell, he thought grimly, I'll never see him again, so what does it matter? But by evening, still nursing the sting of Niko's attack and wanting to settle with him, Gordon rode his bicycle to the harbor and found The Docksider bar by seven o' clock. He walked in and looked around at the swarthy fishermen drinking in the dark bar. Niko was not there.

Gordon decided to have a drink and give him half an hour. At seven-thirty he spoke to the bartender.

"Oh, are you the guy who was supposed to meet him here at seven? Well he told me to tell you he couldn't make it. He's out looking for guys who didn't get back in this morning. Yeah. He left a package for you. Just a sec, I'll get it.'

The bartender came out of the back room behind the bar with a green plastic garbage bag containing something about the size of a football helmet. He handed the bag to Gordon. Gordon looked inside. Whatever was in there was wrapped up in several more bags. Everyone in the bar was now staring curiously at him, and Gordon wanted to leave immediately. "Thanks," he said half-heartedly.

"Don't mention it," said the bartender, walking after Gordon as far as the end of the bar. "Hey, what the hell's in there anyway?"

"I haven't the slightest idea," Gordon replied haughtily.

"Oh yeah, one other thing. Niko said to tell you to make sure you hang it up from the branch of a tree."

Gordon wanted to get home as fast as possible. He had no intention of opening the bag in a public place, for he feared whatever was inside would be disgusting and insulting. The thing looked and felt repulsive, but he had to find out what was inside. The bag was heavy too, it must have weighed about twenty pounds, and Gordon had trouble keeping his balance as he pedaled home with it dangling from the handlebars. He cursed Niko with every pump of the pedals. First he insults me and then he humiliates me, he thought bitterly. What the hell, I only saved his life, what else should I expect?

Panting and sweating as much with anger as with the exertion of the fast ride, Gordon arrived home twenty minutes later. He put the bicycle in the garage and carried the bag around to the back of the house. The sun was setting rapidly but there was still a patch of bright light in the far corner of the yard. Gordon took the bag there and began opening it gingerly, as if it were a bomb. The object inside was wrapped in three bags, one inside the other, and as it rolled out of the last bag with a sickening sucking sound, Gordon was more shocked than if it had been a bomb. Laying on the grass in the sunlight before his feet was the largest conch shell he had ever seen. The shell was iridescent, and, as the sunlight struck it, Gordon was awed by its magical beauty. The conch shell seemed to glow and radiate power, as if it were the greatest treasure stolen from the depths of the ocean, the pearl of the earth. But Gordon's delight changed to confusion: Why did that bastard give me such a beautiful and valuable present? In order to mock me? Out of gratitude for saving his life? Gordon wasn't completely convinced of the latter. There was an animal inside. If Niko had wanted to give me a gift of gratitude, why did he give me a live conch? Then Gordon remembered the instructions to hang it from the branch of a tree. Perhaps there is something more to this mystery, he thought.

The next morning, Gordon woke up at dawn as usual. When he was certain that he was awake, he realized that through the open window was coming the eeriest noise he had ever heard in his life. It sounded like a cat caught in a lawn mower. Pulling on his shorts and strapping on his sandals, he walked through the kitchen out into the backyard. The eerie noise was louder. It was coming from the conch shell which he had tied obediently from a branch of the sycamore tree. The animal was crawling out of its shell, and it was screeching and squealing in its death throes. Gordon felt as if he'd been kicked in the gut. He knelt down on the grass and threw up.

The agonizing death crawl of a conch giving up its shell went on all morning. When Gordon knew it was too late to save the animal, he cleared out of the house and rode his bicycle all over town. Returning home well into the afternoon, he approached the backyard with trepidation. All was quiet there. A magnificently beautiful conch shell was hanging empty from the tree. Gordon looked anxiously around the trunk, but the animal had crawled away into the undergrowth to die.

Gordon could not touch the shell for days, but when it appeared to be thoroughly dried out, he took it into the house and put it on the coffee table. It was a treasure, after all. It was gorgeous to look at. But his pleasant feelings did not carry over to the man who had given him the treasure. Niko had offended him deeply, besides interrupting the flow of his writing, and Gordon felt he deserved an apology.

The following day, the bartender at The Docksider told Gordon what boat Niko was out on and what time it was due in port. Gordon told him what had been in the bag, and the man's eyes popped open with surprise.

Gordon went down to the dock and watched the fishing boats come in. Most of the boats rode deeply submerged, prowing back a heavy furrow of water, and the men who disembarked looked weary but cheerful. It seemed to have been a good day's catch. Niko came walking along in the company of a few other men in raucous good spirits. He was laughing and talking energetically, looking as usual as if he possessed some secret that was the true source of his amusement. When he noticed Gordon staring maliciously at him, he disengaged himself from the group and walked nonchalantly over to him.

"Well, and how did you like my present?"

"It was disgusting and insulting," Gordon blurted out.

"But effective."

"I think you owe me an apology."

"For what? Giving you the most valuable conch shell I've caught in years?" Niko laughed.

"If you wanted to give me a present, why didn't you give me an empty shell?"

"Because the experience of witnessing the animal leaving its shell was part of the present," said Niko seriously.

"What the hell do you mean?"

Niko stared at Gordon, and shifted the harpoon he was carrying from one shoulder to the other. "Well, my young friend, one of the things I could mean is that when you understand what has been sacrificed for something you have greater appreciation for it." He placed his calloused hand on Gordon' s shoulder and harpooned him with his eyes. "But that's not what I mean. I can't tell you what I mean. You must realize it for yourself."

The two men stared at each other. Gordon's face was pale with indignation. He shoved Niko's hand from his shoulder. Niko shrugged at the intended insult and smiled with amusement at his secret and at Gordon's bottled up rage.

"Do you want to hit me? Would that make you feel more like a man?" Niko said sarcastically. "I can see everything you're feeling in your face. I can read you like an open book. You want to hit me, but you haven't got the balls. You've got to toughen up, man. Too much city living has turned you into a candy-ass."

"I should've let you drown."

"What does it matter if I die? My death is only a minor detail. What I don't do this time, I will do next time. And besides, what good would that have done you?"

Gordon turned violently away from Niko and spit viciously into the harbor. "I wish I'd never saved your life."

"I think it's me who's saving yours."

They were alone on the dock now, and they were quiet for a long time. Niko had sat down on a net, to the left of and back-to-back with Gordon, and laid down his harpoon.

"When I was a boy," Niko began, his voice coming from as deep inside him as the past, "I thought my father could touch the sun. And I believed that when I grew up to be a man I too would be able to touch the sun." He paused. "Life is full of disappointments, but only the real ones matter. I like you. And, believe it or not, I am being your friend. You may not recognize it, but you will understand one day how it is I am being your friend now."

Having said all he wanted to say, Niko picked up his harpoon, stood up, and walked away.

The next day, when Dave Gordon went to The Docksider to inquire why Niko hadn't come in on the boats with the others, he was told by the bartender that Niko had gone out on the old boat, the boat had capsized again, and the entire crew was presumed lost. Numbed from the shock, Dave Gordon packed up and returned to New York City that evening.

* * *

When Dave Gordon's first novel was published, many people were puzzled by the dedication: THIS BOOK IS FOR CRAZY NIKO. People thought it odd that such a serious book should have such a lighthearted dedication. One reviewer set a precedent by mentioning a book's dedication for the first time in his column. "This excellent book by a former Times' reporter," the critic wrote, "begins to bewitch the reader not with Chapter One but with the dedication page." Perhaps the most curious and at the same time the most confused, Rita Gordon tried without success to seduce her husband into spilling the beans about who Crazy Niko really was. She ardently felt she had a right to know for two reasons: She believed the book should have been dedicated to her, and she had supported Gordon for most of the time it had taken him to write it. Gordon continually refused to tell her with the explanation that he thought it was bad luck to reveal the identity of his mentor.

The success of his first novel made Gordon's life more complicated. He had always considered the tribulations of writers in the publicity spotlight to be a kind of literary hypochondria. Their complaints were the mere grumblings of prima donnas, nothing to be taken seriously. But Gordon was discovering, after the first thrilling rush of recognition had passed, that publicity was a different process from, always contradicted, and usually destroyed creativity. Now that he had a book in print and had flirted with fame, he was ready to make a lifetime commitment. He wanted nothing more than to begin work on his second novel, and he begrudged every minute that he spent talking to pompous oafs and idiots at the cocktail parties to which his publisher sent him. Gordon now regarded the press with distaste, critics with disdain, and literary parasites with total disgust. He left every party asking himself the same question: What am I doing in New York? The city he had once loved, he now loved and hated.

Rita was behaving rather badly, he thought. She had shown herself to be a poor winner, the kind of person who uses success as a weapon and relishes envy as the greatest revenge. Gordon had a horror of taking her to parties: She drank too much, talked too much, and expected too much. Gordon fared better. Those who managed to engage him in conversation never knew what he was really thinking or feeling, except when he allowed himself to express his open contempt.

One winter night before Christmas, Gordon had had enough. In a silent rage, he threw Rita's fur coat over her shoulders, grabbed her by the arm, and pulled her out the door of an Upper East Side townhouse. Rita still had her drink in her hand half a block away. Gordon snatched it from her and hurtled it into the snow.

"What the hell's the matter with you, I was enjoying myself!"

"You were making an ass of yourself!"

"You're the one who's making an ass of himself with your fucking temper tantrums! You embarrassed the shit out of me in front of some very important people, acting like a goddam primitive."

"I don't give a fuck about important people."

"Well I do. I can stand up to anybody. Not like you. Coward."

"Go to hell."

"And you're a liar, too. You lied to me about being fired from the Times and you lied to me about going to Washington and who the hell knows what else you've lied to me about!"

"I thought I explained all that to you."

"You never explain anything, you only make excuses. I thought maybe success would change you, but you're still the same."

It was snowing and the flakes fell on their dark hair and eyelashes, making them blink but not veiling the malice they bore for one another. The night and the snowstorm locked them together and made them feel the eternity and futility of their struggle. Gordon was struck by the insanity of life, by how men and women sacrificed great passions to petty grudges. Bitterly, he realized that the ultimate power of any individual was the will to self-preservation. This is the way love ends, he thought, at night in the snow with venom on the end of the tongue.

"If you go back to that party, I don't ever want to see you again." And as he said this, Gordon recognized the ultimatum as the fatal blow. Why do I have to test her, push her to the limit, he wondered.

"Then I hope you're gone by the time I get home."

They turned away from each other and walked through the snow in opposite directions. Already Gordon felt colder, and he turned up the collar of his coat.

Satori ✦

A JAPANESE-AMERICAN WOMAN and her husband were staying at the Windsor Hotel on Dominion Square a few steps from the Gare Centrale in downtown Montreal. It was the middle of May and the weather was clear and fine. They knew few people in the city, none to speak of anyway. The man had been there once before, several years prior to his recent marriage, but this was his wife's first visit, and she was quite taken by the city's romantic sophistication.

At 10:07 a.m., in room 715, the Americans were getting ready to go out for the day. The man was counting the money in his wallet, and the woman was checking her hair in the mirror by the door.

"I'd like to stay until Sunday," said the woman, who was used to having her way. "Especially now that the weather is so nice."

"The weather could change," said her husband. "Like New England."

"Weather like this is a gift. Let's enjoy it while we can. Spring is happening all over again."

The man smiled. When his wife put things so delightfully he didn't have the heart to oppose her. He was opening his mouth to say, "Okay, then let's stay a few more days," when he was seized by a sudden fit of violent coughing.

"Are you all right?" Miyako asked, taking a sharp breath.

"The respiratory thing. It's acting up again."

"What about your medication?"

"I left it in New York. Didn't think I'd need it."

"Oh, no. This is a catastrophe. What do you want to do?" Miyako gave him a worried look.

"I'm okay," Andrew said emphatically. "I'll be fine if I don't go out and breathe the air like a damn fool. I'll be fine inside the hotel. I brought a book I've been meaning to read."

"Are you sure?"

"Positive. You go ahead. I'll be fine here. I've got everything I need." Andrew handed her some money. "Take this just in case."

When Miyako had left, Andrew opened a bottle of grapefruit juice and lay down on the unmade bed, stretching and arching his back. The windows faced the square in front of the hotel and the sunlight fell across his legs. He lay there thinking for a while, then got a book from his suitcase and opened it to the first page. The book was a history of the Roman Republic. A few moments later there was a soft knock at the door. When he opened it, he saw one of the housekeepers, a young West Indian woman in a powder blue uniform standing with one hand on a cleaning cart. She did not look at him as she came in. Andrew moved aside and sat at the make-up table while she stripped the bed and straightened up the room. She hummed to herself, absorbed in a dream of her native land, Andrew imagined, as he watched the graceful swaying of her lithe body in the mirror. She worked deftly, her motions effortless, her mind elsewhere,

Andrew thought, oblivious to him; he marveled at her absorption, her swift completion of the work. Through the open door, he heard the song of another housekeeper in the room across the hall, and it struck him how different these women were from his wife. When she finished she left without a word, and the room suddenly lost some of its brightness. She was the kind of woman he had never known, he thought as the door closed and he went back to his reading.

After he had read a page, the door opened again. "I can't leave you here all alone," his wife said as she entered the room.

Andrew remained seated at the make-up table. He sensed it would be better not to say anything. Something was different about her.

"I sat down on a bench in the square," Miyako began, moving to the window and looking out. "I told my legs to get going but they refused." She fell silent. Andrew went over to her and they stood quietly at the window for a while. The sadness left her face suddenly, and she turned around, smiled suggestively, put a hand inside her husband's open shirt, and rubbed the hair on his chest with her fingertips. "What do you suppose we could do in here alone all day?"

A few hours later, after they had made love, slept for half an hour and eaten a lunch of omelettes ordered from room service, Miyako was sitting at the make-up table in a white terrycloth robe and Andrew lay stretched out on the bed sipping a fresh drink of grapefruit juice and vodka. He was reading again but stopped when his wife started brushing her thick, glossy hair. Her hair was so intensely black that it seemed electrically alive, he thought; it seemed to pulsate with life. Everyone in his family had fine light brown hair that lay flat against their heads. He remembered hearing that only Asians and American Indians and maybe Eskimos have true black hair. She brushed it out with long rhythmic strokes, her head tilted back.

"I hope you never cut your hair short," Andrew said.

Miyako smiled. She finished brushing her hair and began to apply her make up. In the eight months of their marriage, Andrew had never seen her go through this process. She dabbed creams from little jars onto her fingertips and rubbed them over her cheeks and forehead, sucking in her cheeks to get at the cheekbones and pausing at intervals to examine her work in the mirror. Picking up a pencil, she drew dark lines on the skin under her eyes, then across the eyelids as she pulled them taut and her jaw dropped down. She painted mascara on her eyelashes. Finally, she plumped up her full lips as though kissing herself in the mirror and daubed on the lipstick, grimacing like a gargoyle in order to stretch her mouth. Recomposed, her face became still again.

"You look stunning," Andrew said. "I don't think I've ever seen you looking more beautiful."

"I love to hear you say that. I hope you never stop saying lovely things like that."

"Promise me that if you ever get the urge to cut your hair you'll tell me first."

Miyako made a fist around her hair and yanked it back. "I want to chop it all off sometimes. Just to see what it feels like." She turned her head to one side and then the other, studying her new face with her hair pulled back. "Do you think you'll ever get tired of me with so many beautiful women in the world?"

"I'll always love you," Andrew replied.

"Even when I'm old?"

"You'll never be old. You're ageless."

Miyako smiled again into the mirror, her brown eyes lighting up. "You always know what to say. That must be why I fell in love with you." She stood up and walked slowly over to the window. The sun shone directly into the square, lighting up the crowd's movement and bright colors. She pressed her knuckles against the glass. "I've just had a top shelf idea," she exclaimed, spinning around. "I'll invite some of those people up here."

"What people?"

"Those people in the square. The jugglers and musicians." Her robe fell to the floor; picking it up, she tossed it over a chair and started getting dressed. "I'll hire them to entertain us."

Andrew was staring at her. "You're serious, aren't you? The room's not big enough."

"Well, the lobby is."

"I don't know, Bije. It's a terrific idea, but . . ." Andrew trailed off.

Fully attired in a summer dress and sandals, Miyako glided swiftly to the door. "Don't worry, I won't get us thrown out of here. I'll ask the directeur for permission."

"Him? Good luck. He makes Caligula look like a boy scout. Why don't you use the phone?"

Miyako looked at Andrew in silence, as if to say he should have known why. "Because I'm much better looking in the eyes than talking in the ear."

She went into the hallway and took the elevator to the lobby. Going up to the marble-topped counter, she told the sullen, plain-looking woman standing behind it that she wished to speak with the directeur. The woman picked up the phone and spoke in French to the manager saying that a guest wanted to see him.

A dark wooden door in the wall behind the counter opened almost immediately and the directeur stepped out. He was smiling benevolently at Miyako, but when she told him what she wanted to do his smile quickly faded and one of his chubby cheeks began to twitch. "I'm afraid such a thing cannot be permitted, madame," he intoned gravely, resting his thick hands on the marble counter. "But if you would allow me, I could suggest an alternative."

"What is it," Miyako asked impatiently.

"I would be delighted to place the salle à manger at your disposal before it opens to the public—providing the entertainment is appropriate." Miyako asked him what he considered appropriate and he continued, his face lighting up. "I know of an excellent chanteuse, a lovely young woman whom your husband would surely find most appealing—"

"No, that wouldn't do," she interrupted. "But a monkey would be nice. You would allow a monkey in our room, wouldn't you?"

The directeur frowned. "Yes, madame, I suppose that would be all right. Providing he's a very small monkey."

"Very good. I saw one out in the square this morning."

Watching Miyako walking across the lobby, the doorman swung the door open for her with a formal nod of his large head. He was an imposing figure in full regalia—a dove-grey uniform with silver buttons in two rows down his broad chest, a cap with an ornate red band—standing erect in the shade of the portico, white-gloved hands at his sides. Miyako took no notice of him.

The square was densely congested with people along its diagonal paths. Miyako smiled, remembering the street fairs she loved as a child in San Francisco's Chinatown. She moved carefully amidst the throng, avoiding all contact with other people. Women shepherded children, young couples embraced, oblivious to the crowd, and old men in dark clothes roosted on benches reading newspapers or talking in the languages of the old world. Well above the heads of the crowd towered the patina-green statue of Jacques Cartier, the French navigator who had named the island Mont Réal, encamped for a day, and then forged ahead into New France. Along the adjacent block to the south, the soot-blackened statues atop the Cathedral of Our Lady, Queen of the World, peered down upon the festivities. Most of the trees in the square, known as Dominion Square, were dogwoods, and they were blossoming in the late Canadian spring. One of the whitish-pink petals drifting down landed in Miyako's hair. She brushed it away without realizing what it was.

Moving along in search of the juggler with the monkey she had seen that morning, she passed artists sketching portraits in charcoal and pastel, and she passed a stout man in a red cap pumping a button accordion while he bellowed out a folk tune in *joual*, the dialect of Quebec. She came to a crowd gathered around a mime. Miyako paused to watch him. He was in a black leotard and white face. With aching slowness, he stretched his body like elastic, extended his arms over his head, and tilted his face upwards in ecstasy. Miyako heard the woman next to her whisper reverentially that he was acting out the life and death of a flower. Enraptured, Miyako watched the mime grow, expand, look up to the sun with gratitude, begin to wilt, shrink, wither, and finally slump down with a face crushed by sadness. Miyako caught her breath sharply, moved by the poignant performance. She felt as though he were her kindred spirit, somehow. As he came around with his hat, she conspicuously tossed in a five-dollar American bill while holding his forearm. "I want to talk with you," she said in breathless French, her eyes lit up. The mime nodded and moved on. When the crowd had thinned out, she went over to him. "You are wonderful!" she exclaimed. The mime nodded and went back to putting his things into a leather bag. Miyako told him that she wanted her husband to see his beautiful performance and explained that he was confined to their hotel room because of his allergies. She pointed up to the seventh floor of the hotel and said that the pollen in the air could trigger a serious attack. "It's awful. His lungs get all clogged up and he can't breathe."

The mime showed little concern. "A private performance of that kind would be quite expensive," he replied.

She asked him how much he would want, and he told her two-hundred dollars. Miyako frowned and said irritably, "That's just too much!"

"I am very sorry you think so," said the mime with offended dignity, returning his attention to packing up his things.

"Is that how much you make giving one of your shows out here?"

He told her it was true and that sometimes he made more than that.

Miyako was vexed. She said she was afraid she could not pay him more than fifty dollars and that was her final offer.

The mime looked away. "I am sorry your husband isn't feeling well. Perhaps tomorrow. . . ?"

"We return to the States tomorrow."

The mime shrugged one shoulder, raised his eyebrows, drew his lips down at the corners, put a worn-out top hat on his head, and walked away. As Miyako watched him go, her body went limp and her shoulders slumped forward. She sank down on the bench and stared at the ground. Her hands began to tremble and her mouth went dry. She was breathing rapidly, and her heart beat faster and faster. She thought she was going to black out. A woman came over and asked her if she was feeling all right, but Miyako did not respond; she kept staring at a piece of broken glass on the ground.

The doorman swung open the heavy door for her; the directeur and the desk clerk exchanged a look of surprise as she crossed the lobby and their eyes followed her until the elevator doors closed. Miyako pressed the button for the seventh floor.

Her husband was lying on his back on the bed, arms behind his head, watching a French television documentary about wild cranes. When the door opened and his wife came into the room, Andrew said, "How'd it go?" without getting a reply but did not realize anything was wrong until Miyako dropped down at the foot of the bed, her head bowed forward and her long black hair making a curtain in front of her face. He jumped up and turned off the set.

There was a long silence, and then Miyako blurted out, "I hate it here! I want to go home!"

Andrew put his arm around her shoulder. "What happened out there, Bije?"

"The world's a nasty place to live."

"It's not so bad," he asserted. "Tell me what happened."

"People are so damned selfish and greedy. They make me sick!" Miyako spoke through clenched teeth. "All they care about is themselves and money, money, money. The almighty dollar rules the world. It's terrible! The world is falling apart. I never really believed it before, but it's true." She was crying, her breath coming in little gasps. "People just don't care about people anymore. Nobody wants to help anybody. I can't live in New York anymore. I've decided that I'm going to quit my job. I want to move upstate and live in an old house with a garden in a small country town where people help each other, and I want to have children and a dog and good friends who come over for dinner on Sundays. . . The world's going to hell, but we can still have that, can't we?"

"You wouldn't be happy doing that for very long, Bije," Andrew said calmly. "You couldn't stand that for more than a week. You know you couldn't."

"Yes, I could," Miyako averred. "I've changed. I'm not the

woman you fell in love with—I'm not the same person you married."

"What happened to you out there?" Andrew repeated. "Are you having some kind of a breakdown?"

"I'm fine. No, I'm not fine. I had a satori. That's what happened. And now everything's changed. A satori changes everything."

"Do you really believe in those?"

"I don't expect you to understand. You have to be Japanese to understand."

"I don't believe that," said Andrew, but as he looked at her he did feel that she was no longer the same. She had passed through some kind of transformation.

"All I can tell you is that I feel different," Miyako said with fear in her voice.

They lay back on the bed and the man cradled his wife in his arms until she fell asleep. Then he went over to the window and looked down at the square, wondering what had come over her and what it would mean when they got back to their lives in New York. Perhaps it would blow over, he thought, but he knew that the sudden illumination the Japanese called "satori" was a serious matter.

It was late afternoon and the crowd in the square had dispersed. Andrew looked down at the tops of the trees misted over with green and yellow buds, noticing that their branches undulated gently in the breeze. For him, those buds held lethal doses of pollen. Occasionally, a car horn penetrated the heavy windows. He was still wondering what could have happened to his wife when someone knocked at the door. Andrew crossed the room and opened it.

The doorman in his dove grey uniform was standing in the hallway with a spider monkey clinging to him. The monkey was wearing a red vest with gold trim and a matching pillbox hat. The doorman's cap was pushed back on his head; the monkey was draped over his left shoulder, one spidery hand gripping an epaulet and his lips around one of the silver buttons running down the man's chest. Beside the doorman stood a waiter behind a cart holding a bowl of nuts and fruit, a bunch of bananas, and a bottle of Mumm's champagne in a bucket of ice.

"The directeur sends all of this for madame," the doorman said, handing the monkey to Andrew. "With his compliments."

Paternity ⚜

A LONG ARM OF desolate beach reached out to the empty horizon on the west side of Block Island Harbor. The light was fading, and the sky had turned to rose and violet. The surface of the water reflected the sky in wavering points of silver that died out as the sky darkened. The ferries from Galilee had stopped running for the day.

Overlooking the harbor stood a big white hotel. On the front porch a man and a woman were finishing their lobster dinner in what remained of the sun. Between them candlelight flickered in a red jar. The day had been hot but the cool air coming in off the Sound riffled the tablecloth and delighted the skin.

"The massacre of the Indians was America's first original sin," the woman said, putting on her straw hat.

"And slavery was the other," the man replied. "But why are you thinking about the Indians?"

"The wooden carvings in the gift shop. They're obscene."

"Well, you and I didn't do anything to them," said the man. "Besides, feeling sorry for them won't help."

"It's just like you to take that attitude. How little you know me. We've been married for five years and you haven't bothered to find out that I'm part Cherokee."

"I thought you were all Irish."

"I'm part Cherokee on my father's side."

"How about that."

"And if more people felt the way I do then maybe something could be done to help them," declared the woman.

"I don't see how," the man replied, pouring what was left of the Chardonnay into their glasses.

"All it takes is guts and gumption, as my grandmomma used to say."

"I wish I'd known her," the man said. "She sounds like quite a character."

"She was wonderful. You would have loved her."

"Not as much as I love you."

The woman touched up her lipstick and the man watched her while he chewed his last bite of food. "Would you like a Grand Marnier?"

"That'd be nice," the woman replied.

The man called the waitress over. "Two Grand Marniers, please."

"Do you want them warmed up?" the waitress asked.

The man looked at the woman.

"Do we?" she inquired.

"Yes, please warm them up," the man told the waitress. "And bring us some coffee."

"May I take these?" asked the waitress, indicating the plates of lobster shells.

"We're finished," said the man, and the waitress cleared the table.

"Do you like working here?" the woman asked her.

"The money's good," she answered without looking at either of them. "It helps pay my tuition."

"My husband and I are teachers."

"Oh, really? Where?"

"UMass. My specialty is the Italian Renaissance," the man said simply.

"I teach high school English," added the woman. "We both worked our way through college."

The waitress nodded and left to get their drinks.

"I don't think she's particularly interested in us," said the man.

"Just being friendly."

After a pause the man said, "We need to talk about what we're doing this summer. I'd like to spend a month in Florence. We didn't go last year and I need to do a little research . . . Are you listening to me?"

"He must be three," the woman said, watching a boy walk along the harbor with his parents. "Marco would have been three this year."

"We shouldn't talk about Marco anymore."

They were quiet. The woman looked at the fading colors of the sky. The waitress came over with their drinks and the man told her she could bring the check whenever she was ready.

"Are you all right, Lee?"

The woman shook her head. "Not really, no."

"Have some Grand Marnier. It'll make you feel better."

"I doubt it."

"I should have known something wasn't right," said the woman after a long pause. I should have known from the way he was kicking."

"It wasn't your fault. It wasn't meant to be, that's all."

"That doesn't change the way I feel. He was so close. A few

more pushes and he would have been out."

"Don't torture yourself, Lee. It wasn't meant to be. You've got to resign yourself to that, or at least be more philosophical about it."

"How can I be philosophical about losing a baby?" the woman retorted sharply.

"I think it's time for us to try again," said the man after a pause.

"I don't know about that. I don't think I'm ready for that." The woman sipped her drink and watched the boats in the harbor. She took another sip and coughed.

"Are you all right?"

"I'm fine." She coughed again.

"Drink some water," said the man.

The woman drank some water. "I'm fine now," she said.

Taking his wife's hand, the man looked steadily into her blue eyes. "This may not be the right time to talk about it but it's been on my mind for quite a while. I'd like to have another child, Lee."

The woman looked away. "That wouldn't be prudent," she replied.

"Why not?"

"It wouldn't. It just wouldn't."

"Please give me a reason."

"I'm not ready to risk what happened to Marco again."

"It's highly unlikely the same thing will happen next time. The doctor said it was a freak accident."

"What does the doctor know? If he knew anything it would never have happened in the first place."

"You don't know that for sure. I was there, remember? It was an accident. Tragically unfortunate, but an accident. Nothing more."

"I don't understand how an accident like that could have happened. You'll never convince me it was an accident. They should have known the cord was wrapped around his neck. How could they not have known?"

The man looked out to the horizon and took a long swallow of his Grand Marnier. "That's a question we can never answer," he said at last.

The woman got up from the table and walked to the other end of the porch. All the other diners had left and she stood among the empty tables looking out at the Sound with her hands clutching the back of a chair. The ghostly silhouette of a late incoming sailboat glided along the horizon. The almost-full moon, which had been out early, had floated higher up into the sky. It looked like a translucent wafer that reminded her of the communion host. The sea was no longer deep blue. It had turned stone gray and was on its way to black.

"We're luckier than most people," the woman said when she got back to the table. "We have our health and we both have decent jobs."

"And love," said the man. "Let's not forget about love."

"I love you, Darryl, but I don't think I have the strength to give you what you want." She paused. "Couldn't we adopt?"

"We could. But it's not the same. It wouldn't vindicate Marco."

"You mean you wouldn't be transmitting your genes to the next generation."

"Something like that."

"Does passing on your own individual DNA really matter anymore?"

"Yes. It matters to me," the man replied firmly. "I don't know why exactly, but I can't bear the thought of not leaving something of myself behind."

"You leave your stamp on the minds of the young people in your classes, don't you? Isn't that enough?"

"No, it's not. Whatever this is it's primal. It comes from here," he stated, striking his gut.

"Why not from there?" the woman queried, indicating her husband's forehead.

"No doubt my ego's also involved," the man answered. "I'll grant you that. But regardless of where it comes from it's real. And it's very strong."

The woman remained silent, watching the boy and the two adults until they were out of sight.

"What happens if I can't?"

"We won't know until we try."

"What happens if I won't?"

"Why wouldn't you? Eventually, I mean."

The woman turned away. "Eventually? I guess anything is possible when you look at it that way."

"There's nothing to be afraid of, Lee. You know I'll love you whatever happens."

"I don't believe that. You only love me as long as I give you what you want."

"That's so unfair."

"It's the truth."

"It's your version." The man paused. "All right. Forget about it. Let's just see what happens. I can't make you change your mind but you may feel differently about it in a while."

The woman looked at him shrewdly. "Don't count on any age alarm going off. Not all women have a biological time clock built in."

"We'll see about that."

"I don't appreciate your mechanistic view, if that's what it is. Just because I'm slightly over thirty doesn't mean you can scare me into getting pregnant again."

"I'm not trying to scare you into anything. I'm just biding my time."

"Hah! I won't stop taking my birth control pills."

"Fine. If that's what you want."

"And you won't be allowed near me without a condom!"

"As you wish."

"Don't patronize me." Her eyes glinting, the woman smiled wickedly. "I'll have my tubes tied. That'll fix your wagon."

"Please calm down. This is getting way out of hand." The man stood up. "I want another drink. Would you like one?"

"Sure, why not. I wouldn't want to spoil our weekend. We were having such a nice time."

The man went into the restaurant and ordered two more drinks from the woman behind the bar.

His wife watched him through the big front window. She saw the barmaid smile warmly at him and laugh at something he said. She turned around to face the blackened Sound, lacquered now with moonlight.

As the man was waiting for the drinks, he glanced at the old men sitting at the bar. They were sullenly drinking, their eyes fixed to a baseball game on the television screen. He paid for the two Grand Marniers and walked with them out to the porch where his wife was waiting. She looked up at him as he sat down.

"If I give you what you want will you be happy?" she asked with a sardonic smile.

"You know I will," the man replied, noticing that the candle had gone out.

"And you'll never leave me?" asked the woman, a pained expression on her shadowed face.

"You're much too precious to me, Leah."

"Because if you do I promise you'll never see your children again."

"I don't believe you," said the man.

A Very Good Year ✤

RUE GUILBAULT WAS dark and tunnel-like but enough streetlamp light filtered in from Boulevard Saint Laurent for the young American to see the snow piling up on the ice-covered street, sidewalks and exterior staircase to his apartment building. He was standing outside on a ledge-like balcony feeling the stillness and looking at the glow in the sky over the city. The snow-hush had settled into the large cold-water flat in the heart of Montreal where a young English woman was reclining on a grass-green sofa next to the gas space heater that stood against the wall in the living room. Their angora cat stretched herself near the young woman's belly.

"How does it look?" the young woman asked, lifting her green eyes from the page she was reading as the American entered the room.

"Quiet and steady," the young man replied, replacing the rolled-up blanket against the double doors to the balcony. "It won't quit till we're good and buried."

"Perhaps it won't be that bad."

The man smirked. "I can read the signs. This is a bad one."

The young woman closed her eyes and sighed. "I'm glad you're going to New York on Monday."

"I'll go if the airport's open."

"Pity you won't take the train. The train would take longer."

"You would have to say that."

"I didn't mean it that way. I meant it would be nice for you if you were away for a few more days."

The young man shrugged. "A few more days . . ."

"This happens to you every year about this time. You go a little stir crazy, as you Americans say."

"It's much more serious than that."

The young woman stroked the cat with her right hand, pressing it against her. Her left hand dangled the book she was reading, Flaubert's *A Sentimental Education*, with her forefinger marking the page. "Please don't ask me what I think you're about to ask me."

The young man looked down at his hands. "I hate living like this," he said. "We don't deserve to live like this. We don't belong here."

"I'm not ready to go back to England," she said.

"And I'm not ready to go back to the States. But it's time for us to leave Montreal."

"Where do you intend for us to go?"

"France," said the young man with determination in his voice.

"France would certainly be nice but why can't you be happy right here in Canada?"

"I'd be much happier in Paris."

"That's what you say now."

"I've never been more sure of anything in my life. I want our baby to be born in Paris."

"What's wrong with our baby being born in Montreal? We

have good friends here. I don't want to start up all over again, getting to know people and finding work and all that bother. I want to get married and give this baby a stable home. This is really no time to go to Paris."

"Why not? We know a few people there already. It won't take long to make new friends."

"Maybe not but how will we live there? What will we live on—our friends?"

"I'll get regular assignments from that magazine in New York."

"That sounds splendid, darling, and I believe it's possible because I know you're good enough. But what happens if you don't get regular assignments? What happens if they don't like your work?"

"They'll like my work. I'm sure of it. And if they don't I'll write for some other magazine."

"What other magazine?"

"I don't know offhand, but if necessary I'll teach English at Berlitz. I'll play my violin on the streets. I'll do whatever it takes. Why can't you have more faith in me?"

The woman stood up from the sofa. She was tall and her flaxen hair fell loosely over her shoulders. She pulled at her fisherknit sweater, a gift from her parents after a visit to the Isle of Aran, and stretched it down over her belly and hips. The man looked at the indentation in the sofa cushions expecting the hollows to fill in again.

"I have every reason to complain," the woman said in a strained voice. "Living the way we do isn't easy for me."

The young English woman walked down the hallway to the bedroom. She lay down on the bed without turning on the light. The tears came, and she waited for the American but he didn't come to her. After a while of waiting she got up, stripped the quilt from the bed, wrapped it around herself, and went out on the back porch. The quilt was a birthday present from her grandmother in Devon, England; it was thick and sturdy and kept out the damp cold of this city on an island in the Saint Lawrence River. The snow was falling heavily in the courtyard. The young woman watched the flakes swirling in the dim light from many naked bulbs.

An old woman who lived alone in the building next door had also come out on her back porch. The old woman put out a wrinkled hand and let the flakes fall into her palm. The young woman watched her in the pale light from the bulbs that were never turned off on the back porches. She was dressed in a heavy army parka with the hood up over her frail head and the strings pulled tight around her oval face. Her right hand gripped the porch railing, and her legs in their baggy pants seemed to bend at the knees.

The young woman hurried back inside the apartment, draping the quilt over the back of a kitchen chair. She filled the kettle and placed it on the stove to boil water for tea. The young man came into the kitchen.

"That old woman gives me the creeps," the young woman said with a shudder.

"Which old woman?"

"In the building on the other side of the courtyard."

The young man went out on the back porch and came back in again. "All she's doing is looking at the snow."

"She was watching me."

The young man took her in his arms. "I love you," he said. "And I'll love baby."

"Will you? I'm not so sure. I think you'd rather not have one. A baby is the last thing you need right now."

The young man looked down at the drain in the sink. A blue-green streak stained the white porcelain. He tightened the faucet and the thin stream of water ceased flowing.

"I wished we'd never come up here," the young woman said. "Everything started to go wrong up here."

"You really were happier in Boston, weren't you?"

"I was much happier in Boston because you were much happier in Boston." She looked at the filmy light from the naked bulbs in the courtyard. "I know I'm not very independent, but I can't help it. You affect me that way. I can't be happy unless you're happy."

"That first year was a very good year," the young man said with a smile. "I can remember the first time I saw you. I thought I'd never seen a more beautiful woman. I was shaking, but I had to speak with you. I knew I'd never get another chance."

The young woman was also smiling. "I thought you were very suave."

"Suave? On the outside maybe."

"It took a lot of nerve to come up to a strange woman in a bookstore, begin a conversation, and ask her out to lunch. I was very impressed."

"It took a lot of nerve to move in with me three months later," the young man said.

The young woman's eyes filled with light "I loved that apartment we lived in on Marlborough Street. I loved the way the light came through the living room windows."

"And going up on the roof, and looking at the river. And making love up there in the rain. I loved that."

"We were so happy there."

"That was a very good year," the young American man said.

Their smiles faded, and they were quiet, looking out from the dark kitchen and watching the snow falling luminously in the courtyard.

"Maybe you should stay in New York for a while," the young woman said. "You've got friends there. Maybe you should stay with them until you work this out."

"We have to stay together to work this out."

"You know what I mean. A little time away from each other would do us a world of good. You might learn to appreciate me more."

"I do appreciate you. Just because you say I don't appreciate you doesn't mean I don't."

"I don't think you want this baby. I don't think you love me anymore."

"That's just crazy. If I didn't love you anymore I wouldn't stay with you."

"Then why won't you marry me?"

"Because marriage would change everything."

"How would it change everything?"

"It would change the way we look at life. I wouldn't feel free."

"And feeling free you stay with me, is that it?"

"Yeah, I guess that's it. Weird paradox, isn't it?" The young man took the young woman in his arms again and kissed her lips and throat. She did not press her body against his.

"We could ask my parents for a loan to help us get set up in Paris," she said over his shoulder. "They've got lots of money."

The young man let go of her. "I don't want to do that."

"They'd give it to us as a wedding present."

"If we ever do get married it won't be because of your parents' money."

"I'm sorry, darling. I didn't mean it that way." She turned off the burner under the kettle and watched the plume of steam die down. "You don't have to stay with me because of this baby," she said quietly. "I'm quite capable of raising her on my own."

"I know you are."

"And you're perfectly capable of going to Paris alone."

"Yes, that's true."

The young English woman picked up the quilt, threw it over her shoulders, and went out on the back porch.

The young man took a bottle of cognac from a cabinet and poured some into a glass. He stood at the kitchen table, taking a long swallow of the amber liquid and looking at the back door with its matching panes of narrow glass and its thick yellowish surface of many-layered coats of paint. His eyes moved to the dishes in the drain, the dull pots hanging from the yellow pegboard, the jars of spices in their rack on the wall, and the dusty silk lilies in their ceramic vase on the table. He glanced up at the calendar and looked at the bad reproduction of the Pissarro landscape hanging frameless beside it. Then he opened the back door and said, "How are you doing?"

"Terrible," the young woman replied. "I'm cold and I could use a drink."

The young man stepped outside. "What about the baby?"

"Yes, I suppose I shouldn't."

"Why don't you come back inside," he suggested.

She looked up at him. "It really doesn't matter where we live, as long as you love me. You do love me, don't you?"

The young man took both her hands and helped her to stand. "Absolutely, I love you," he said, looking into her eyes. "It's just our life I want to change."

In The Rockies ⚜

MY NAME IS Sylvester and this is a true story. Honest. I want it to be the most honest story you'll ever read. I should know if it's true or not because it happened to me and my wife. Her name is Jessica. She has long blonde hair, sparkling green eyes and a sensuous body. Solid Celtic good looks. Except that she's too tall, too tall for me anyway, but then I'm only of average height. I wish I were taller by a few inches but that's another matter. I think that the root of Jessie's problems is that she is just too big, and she wants life to be big, wants people to be bigger than life. She is often deceived or disappointed. And what she can't find in life she looks for in books. She reads a lot.

It was her idea to hitchhike back from Vancouver to Montreal. I wanted to take the train, but we didn't have enough money left for the train and so really had no choice. But Jessie had always been for hitching, and she was thrilled to be setting out on another adventure.

We had no problem getting a ride—Jessie's figure and flag of blonde hair saw to that—until we got into the country. Our last ride, an Okanogan Valley hippie-farmess-cum-religious-fanatic, dropped us off in her small town. We had a beer with her in the local saloon and headed out on the highway. It was late evening and the sun spangled the tops of the humpy hills. The spaces between the hills ever filling with cold shadows. The sun was setting over the plains, night was drawing nigh, and the highway looked emptier and emptier. Desolate is the right word to describe it. Not even Jessie's figure could lure the few pickups and even fewer cars roaring around the curve that exited from the highway just before it stretched out its long reach towards the Rockies. Finally Jessie sat down on her packsack and turned her back to the road with a shrug of obstinate anger. This worried me. When Jessie gives her back to something then I know it's hopeless.

"Com'on, Jessie," I implored. I wanted her flag of hair blowing in the now chilly breeze.

"No," she answered flatly, staring out over the hills as though expecting the cavalry on the horizon. "I think we should go back to that saloon and get a room for the night."

I didn't like that idea at all. I wasn't too crazy about the way one of the ranchers in there had been ogling her. "Let's give it a while. It's too early to quit now. We haven't gone far enough. Come and help me with this thing, will ya?" I was fumbling with the broken strap of my backpack.

Jessie came over and took command of the operation. We were both bent over, she tying the maddening strap back on, when a truck roared around the corner, passed by the exit and headed out on the open highway. We stood up in time to see it stop. It waited while we gathered up our gear and bolted.

Jessie hopped in front. I opened the side door and jumped in back. No sooner were we inside than the truck, an old Chevy carry-all, was off again, lurching forward as the gears were shifted. It happened so fast that I hardly had time to think—or take a look at our driver. One minute we had been stranded on the side of the road and the next I was watching the tops of the humpy hills roll past from the floor of a Chevy carry-all. The driver—I could only see the back of his head and shoulders—looked about twenty-six. He had shortish light-brown hair and was wearing a flannel shirt. Jessie was being her most effusive, trying to engage him in conversation (she preferred to sit in front and always felt obliged to make conversation), but he simply did not want to talk. I guess he just wanted company, the presence of other people on the long and lonely ride. He tried to be friendly—it was near impossible to be unfriendly with Jessie—but the man was hampered by a horrendous cold and kept sneezing and blowing his nose while Jessie held the wheel.

I took in my immediate surroundings. It wasn't just a truck, it was a house on wheels. Plywood cabinets and shelves were built in around a stove and refrigerator. There were curtains on the windows, a carpet on the floor and camel bells hanging from the back doors. In addition to my own gear, there was another backpack and a guitar. But to top things off, there were two photographs tacked up on the plywood paneling facing each other: one was of Roy Rogers (hat tilted back, white neck-scarf, broad grin) and the other a reproduction of a painting of the Hindu god Krishna clipped from a magazine.

We drove along in almost total silence (except for the camel bells), catching up to the darkness and watching the rose sunset recede. At ten we pulled into Penticton, a resort town on a lake in British Columbia. This much information had Jessie pried from the silent, anonymous driver: he was spending the night at his girlfriend's house in this town and tomorrow would be continuing his journey east. Stepping out of the truck, expressing our gratitude. He said off-handedly: "I'll be leaving about eleven tomorrow. If I see you out on the highway I'll pick you up."

"That'd be great," I said, thinking it would be the most unlikely thing in the world.

The next morning, warm and beautiful, our first ride was a short one out of town with a fiftyish man who owned a glider business. Once again we were stranded out on the highway. We started walking and kept going for miles. No one stopped. No one. And this time we had competition. We were forced to keep walking in order to stay ahead of the half-dozen or so other hitchers strung out along the safe stopping areas. About noon we were exhausted. Jessie complained volubly but I willed her on, believing our chances would be better the more we increased our lead from the others. We talked about the man with the cold and the unlikeliness of seeing him again, but still it kept us hoping. And walking. Finally, our feet just gave out—Jessie's feet. She just stopped flopped down by the side of the road and refused to budge—in fact, she fell asleep. At last, I too succumbed to exhaustion and took a nap.

Fifteen minutes later I awakened and stood up, and no sooner had I done it than what should I see coming along the road but the very same Chevy carry-all. Not believing my eyes, I shouted to Jessie. She woke up and saw it too. We waved. It stopped. There must have been five people inside. There were. Three of them jumped out of the back, dragging their packsacks with them. I heard the man with the cold calling after them, "Like I told you, I promised these people a ride last night."

I could hardly believe what was happening. I didn't think the hospitality of the road extended this far. The ousted hitchers grumbled as they took up our post on the highway and we took up theirs in the now familiar house on wheels with the pictures of Roy Rogers and Krishna staring beneficently down at us. The truck lurched off and we settled back for a long ride.

There were two new additions to our "family," the man's girlfriend and her small mutt. The man's girlfriend turned out to be affable and motherly, as long-winded as her boyfriend was silent. Unfortunately, she and Jessie could not agree on a topic for conversation. She said they were headed for Winnipeg, and we could travel all the way with them if we liked. We were delighted. Hours later the homey truck was filled with a relaxed silence. Jessie took out a book and settled in for a long read. The woman put a tape into the tape-deck. It turned out to be one of the most unlikely combinations of music in a day of unlikely occurrences: country & western, Buddhist chanting and George Har-rison. It played over and over again, turned out to be the only tape they had, and every time "Apple Schruffs" came on the dog howled along with the harmonica.

And the camel bells tinkled their very own tune.

And Roy Rogers smiled his wholesome cowboy smile.

And Krishna smiled his enigmatic, mystical smile.

And the miles kept rolling on by.

That evening we passed into the magnificent Rockies and stopped at Canmore, a small town just east of Banff National Park, where our hosts were delivering a basket of Okanogan Valley peaches to a friend. We all jumped out to stretch our legs. Jessie, being Jessie, headed straight for the local grocery store attached to the gas station where we had pulled up.

Another woman was coming out of the store just as Jessie was entering. They ran into each other. They couldn't avoid it. Jessie looked up. The other woman looked up. Ensued shrieks of delight and much hugging. The other woman was a lovely blonde, an old friend from Montreal, an actress with whom Jessie had worked in the theatre and after whom I had lusted. I was called over to share in the marveling over coincidence and the rush of words to explain and sort out the details. I watched the faces of my wife and Susan flushed and exuberant in the mauve dusk with the heavy-shouldered mountains darkly behind.

In the excitement we'd forgotten our hosts who were now sitting in the cab of their truck, the peaches undelivered to their absent friend, waiting patiently for us to rejoin them. Susan hurriedly invited us to spend a few days with her and Aaron in their cabin across the way. A quick conference followed between Jessie and myself. We accepted. Moments later, we were walking on either side of Susan, our gear on our backs, while the Chevy carry-all disappeared into the vanishing point. The next occupants of that house on wheels would rest comfortably and gratefully under the benign smiles of Roy Rogers and Krishna.

We stood by the open road, waiting for a break in the traffic. The cabin which blonde-haired blue-eyed Susan of German lineage and perpetually rosy cheeks was sharing with her Jewish lover, Aaron, was five-hundred yards away under the trees at the edge of an open field.

We crossed the highway and struck out across the field.

"Aaron will be so surprised to see you. Really," Susan enthused. Our long shadows going in front of us. I noticing Susan's lithe and supple body beneath her Indian cotton shirt and filling her jeans. Watching her white-blonde hair flashing like a mane.

"It's just incredible meeting you here in the mountains," said Jessie. "I just can't believe it."

"Neither will Aaron," Susan answered, coming up to the cabin and opening the door. "Aaron! Guess who I found."

It was semi-dark inside the cabin, a cave of twilight. Aaron a shape and voice from the bed, a man adrift in a pleasant reverie jerked back into reality. Baffled. Lying on back, head lifted, struggling to sit up, to confront three intruders who crowded into the single room.

"You can't come here, I'm hiding," he said, regaining presence of mind, an actor's mind, reflexes finely tuned. "How did you find me?" swinging his shortish legs off the bed and lifting his barrel-chested body erect in one smooth movement. Coming to me and shaking my hand manfully. "You putz, how did you find me here?" His hair ruffled, eyes twinkling, beard unkempt from days in the mountains, he looked like a dwarf out of a fairy-tale.

"Hello, Aaron, you old wandering Jew."

But he had already turned to Jessie and was hugging and kissing her in his erotic-impersonal theatrical way. "You're looking very lovely," he said. "So what happened," he asked Susan with boyish bewilderment.

Susan told him.

"This is fantastic," Aaron summing up his feelings. Wearing only a pair of army fatigues, he padded around rubbing his curly-haired chest and protuberant belly, savoring the moment, lighting a cigarette, turning on lights, setting the stage.

Jessie and I stored our gear and made ourselves at home. While Susan and Jessie made tea, Aaron and I started in on a bottle of whiskey and a pack of cigarettes.

The room was furnished with a double bed, sofa, chairs, divided into a bedroom and a kitchen, very homey. Isolated in the mountains, it was the kind of place that demanded intimacy among people. Aaron was not a person I wanted myself or Jessie being intimate with. I never completely trusted him, and I never could decide whether I liked him or not.

Aaron and Susan had left Montreal in an old Volkswagen a week earlier and were heading out for Vancouver and a new life.

Theirs was a passionate and earthy relationship. Demanded movement, action, travel. In sharp contrast to Jessie and mine; ours a cool, romanticized desire, theirs a fiery, consuming one. Sex for Jessie and me was tender and polite. Aaron and Susan made an egomaniacal display of their overwhelming desire for each other. They were explorers, we were settlers.

We smoked, drank from the bottle of whiskey and talked until dawn which comes late in the mountains. The sky was indigo blue when we went to sleep.

In the morning, Susan cooked breakfast: eggs, sausages and home fried potatoes. Aaron ritualistically performed his job, making a pot of coffee. Outside the sun shone clean and bright; the mountains loomed majestically, their peaks a faraway world cloaked in mists. I expected something to happen here, in the mountains. Aaron was a masterful psychological gamesman— he'd tried in Montreal to knife his way into my libido—and Susan was a Siren. Maybe Jessie would be victim.

We each made a trip out to the bathrooms sequestered among the trees then sat down to the good country breakfast.

Jessie was bright and cheerful like the day outside. "I saw a rabbit on my way down to the bathroom."

"Did you?" said Aaron, crunching down on a slice of toast. "There're all kinds of animals around here. Elk, mountain goats . . . bears." His eyes twinkled with mischief.

"Oh, Aaron, there aren't any bears down this far," Susan debunked. "You're just trying to scare her."

"I'm not scared," Jessie piped up. "I'd love to see a bear. I hope we can see some."

"I've seen a whole family of black bears."

"Oh, Aaron, where?"

"Down past the field with the wild horses."

"Wild horses?" exclaimed Jessie. "Can we see them too?"

"Certainly," Aaron smug, looking up from his plate, fork poised, "unless they've made themselves invisible again."

After breakfast we all trooped out along a path through high grass, across railroad tracks and into wooded fields overgrown with weeds and bushes and alive with hurrying, toiling insects. Aaron led the way. It was hot and insect-loud. He made a slight detour to show us an old abandoned cabin he'd found. At last we climbed through barbed wire and stood up in a horse-bitten field of stubble.

"This is where their territory begins," Aaron proclaimed dramatically.

"Are they dangerous?" asked Jessie. She wanted them to be.

"They're totally unpredictable. We'll have to walk out in the open so we don't come on them suddenly."

A current of tension shot through us.

"We don't want to spook them," added Susan, lips pursed, wearing her white-blonde hair in braids, blue eyes alert behind wire-rimmed glasses. I just then realized she had one of the sultriest voices I'd ever heard.

The field was open for about fifty yards, then dropped to a pocket of shrub and bush. Aaron moved cautiously towards this pocket, from where we all expected the horses to bolt at any moment. Following Aaron, we each instinctively chose our path of safest entry, entered the pocket and walked through it for another twenty feet. Then we came out into a smaller, secluded clearing like a natural corral.

And there were the horses, two of them, a white Welsh mare and a bay quarter-horse with black mane and tail, tense, eyeing us intensely. We stopped dead. Then Aaron stepped towards them speaking softly and holding out his hand, but the horses skittered a few steps away, the bay hoofing the ground and neighing deep in his throat.

"They don't look wild to me," I scoffed, "just scared."

"No one can get near them, except Aaron," said Susan.

But Aaron was having a very difficult time of it. He was about twenty-five feet ahead of us, holding out his hand and calling gently. The horses starting circling the clearing, heads lowered and ears pricked up, and the bay was still whinnying threateningly.

Susan was worried. "Don't go any closer, Aaron" she called.

"I think we'd better leave them alone," Jessie chimed in.

Aaron ignored their warnings and relentlessly closed in on the horses. At the last moment, when Aaron was within a few feet and I was sure the horses would rear up and trample him, they swung around and trotted off through an opening in the other end of the clearing.

"They got away," said Aaron as we came up to him. If it were a game he was playing, it was a more dangerous one than I had expected.

Susan and Jessie were exhilarated by this display. Susan hugged Aaron tightly, as though he'd been snatched from the jaws of death. Excitement was written all over Jessie's face.

I asserted myself the only way I could, with sarcasm. "So these are your wild horses, eh?"

Aaron only beamed at me with self-satisfied conceit, over Susan's shoulder.

We walked down to a river, which was glacier-fed and too cold for swimming. The day was hot, and Aaron and I peeled off our shirts and bared our chests to the sun. The women teasingly threatened to do the same.

"This is where I saw the bears," Aaron announced.

We looked around, at grass, trees, mountains, all drenched in sunshine, but no bears. No one really cared to see bears after the encounter with the horses. Not even Jessie. She was investigating an impromptu bridge made of trees and boards that had collapsed into the river. I went down to the bank and played lifeguard. Turning around, I saw Aaron and Susan disappearing into the woods and experienced a pang of envy.

That evening Jessie and I decided to stay on a few days and we rented a cabin of our own. We talked as we set up house.

"I thought that stunt Aaron pulled with the horses was very stupid. He could have been trampled to death." I was unpacking my things, shrugging off the road-weariness.

Jessie, inspecting the kitchen, setting life in temporary order. "Maybe. But I thought it was fun at the time."

"He and Susan, they're both ego-maniacs. I never could put up with the games they played in Montreal."

"Please don't start bitching, Sylvester." Jessie at the window, adjusting the curtains, letting in more light. "It's our vacation and I want to enjoy myself. You can leave if you want, but I'm staying for a while."

"It's just that I can't stand the way they're always acting." I drifted off, my point sounding weak and petty.

"Who says they're acting?" The screen door slammed behind her.

I caught a glimpse of her blonde hair as she passed by the bedroom window. Alone in the cabin I suddenly felt more restless than I'd ever felt on the road. Jessie made herself at home everywhere, with everyone. She made the best of what she had, while I destroyed what didn't fit in with what I wanted. The cabin seemed empty without her.

Fifteen minutes later Jessie came back with a handful of wildflowers: daisies, bluebells, buttercups, a riot of color. She found an old jar, filled it with water and arranged the flowers on the table in front of the window, then stood back to admire her work.

Standing by her side I turned her around and kissed her. Passion flared up in me. "Let's make love."

Jessie turned away. "Not now, there's too much work to do. Besides, you're only turned on because of Aaron and Susan."

She'd hit the nail on the head. "So what if I am? What's wrong with that? It's you I want, not her."

"I'm not so sure about that."

"Well *I* am." I caressed her shoulders.

"Please don't.

"I want you, Jess."

"I wish I could believe that."

"What are you talking about? Just because there've been other women doesn't mean that every time. . . . " I regretted having always told her everything. She stepped away from me over to the sink and began washing her hands.

"Well, anyway I'm just not turned on right now. Please try to understand that." The formality in her tone hurt as much as the rejection and the implication that I could only make love to her while thinking of someone else.

"Maybe you're right,"—me, resentful—"maybe our sex life has become so fucking stale that I need other women to excite me."

"That's fine. Maybe I need other men." A last thrust from Jessie as I was about to let the screen door slam behind me.

The sunshine mantled the mountains in a golden evening light. No one else was about, most of the other cabins being empty. I needed to clear my head. Instinctively, I took the path we had taken that afternoon and walked into the fields with the wild horses, straight through the pocket of shrub and bush into the inner clearing. I was disappointed. There were no horses, just a flock of big black mountain crows that lifted up like bits of shadow and settled into the tall trees above my head, caw-

cawing in those weirdly human-like voices. I threw a few stones
at them but they refused to budge.

I pushed through the bush at the other side of the clearing,
on my way to the river. And there they were, right in front of
me. The two wild horses being fed from the hands of a teen-age
boy and girl. When I stepped out the horses skittered away
about twenty yards and started munching the grass.

"Are those horses wild?" I demanded.

The boy and girl looked at me like I was crazy. Their startled
faces gave me the answer I wanted. "They're just a little
nervous, mister, that's all," said the boy.

"I'm sorry," I said. I turned around and headed back towards
the cabins. Before, I wasn't sure if I liked Aaron or not, now I
was certain that I despised him. He'd deceived us all, and I was
determined to get even by exposing his fraudulent manhood and
reasserting my genuine one.

I crossed the railroad tracks, walked through the tall grass for
another fifty feet and came out on the mown lawn behind the
outhouse. I heard the toilet flush and, as I walked closer, the
door close on the other side. Turning the corner, I came face to
face with Aaron. The darkness did not hide my anger.

"Just had a good shit." Aaron never lost his presence of
mind. "Looks like you've been out walking."

"Yeah, I've been out bear hunting," I retorted with all the
sarcasm I could muster.

Aaron's eyes twinkled. He rubbed his belly and smiled that
enigmatic, mystical Krishna smile I'd seen on the picture in the
back of the Chevy truck. It really was uncanny, the similarity
between those smiles.

He put his arm around my shoulder and urged me along a
few paces before he said, "You'd like to fuck my old lady,
wouldn't you?"

I answered without missing a beat. "Yeah, I would."

"You're welcome to try." He smiled that smile again.

I admired his command of the situation, but I didn't trust him for one moment. He knew exactly where to thrust the dagger, if I let him. "Are you so sure I'd fail?" It was lame, but it was the best I could do.

His only answer was to remove his arm from my shoulder. We walked along in silence for a few more paces, stopping in front of his cabin. I imagined Susan inside, getting dinner ready.

"It seems like you're having some kind of trouble with Jessica. Want to talk about it?"

I looked up keenly, warily, probing his face in the twilight darkness for a clue to his real motive, his real feelings. All I could see was that same uncanny Krishna smile until it seemed to loom as formidably as the mountains behind. I stared into his penetrating, twinkling eyes until they seemed to become as knowing as the eyes of life itself.

"I don't think it's any of your business."

"I make it my business when my friends are unhappy." It sounded like a line from one of his stage roles. Suddenly, he took my head between his hands and kissed me on the forehead. "I love your genius," he said.

Despite my anger a smile streaked across my face, a lopsided, wholesome smile, just spilling out of me against my volition.

Then I turned and walked away. When I was half-way down the path to my cabin, Aaron called me. I turned around, saw him standing with his hand on his door.

"The world wants to be deceived," he said.

A New Path ✦

SEATED AT HIS drawing board, Clayton Simonelli heard the sound of his wife's mellifluous voice and his son's piping staccato as he answered her. Both of his children were in the kitchen with Eleanor having juice. They had just come in from playing in the yard. It was after 7:00 on an evening in August, and they would be going up to bed soon. He listened to their voices and wished he could be with them, but he still had work to do.

Clayton smelled the fragrance of grass and wildflowers that came in through the open window. He was having trouble concentrating. He looked at the things on his walls: his MFA from the Rhode Island School of Design, snapshots of a trip to Europe, books on the history of art and architecture, a photo of Frank Lloyd Wright and a print of a self-portrait of his hero, Leonardo DaVinci. Spears of sunlight revealed the dust that had accumulated on them.

His workroom was on the first floor and jutted out to the side. This was the remotest and quietest place in the house, which he had designed himself. From the windows, he could view the Farmington River and survey a yard that sloped smoothly for 500 feet to a scattering of trees and a pond where a pair of Canadian geese make their summer home. At forty-two, he finally had the house and the property he had always wanted. Now all he needed was the time to enjoy them. He put Alain Stivel's "Renaissance of the Celtic Harp" into the player and studied the drawing on the board. Then he examined his Rapidiograph pens. The one that was the right size had to be cleaned.

The workroom door opened and an auburn-haired blue-eyed child looked in. "Da!" Erica exclaimed with monosyllabic poetry as she toddled over to him. Clayton lifted her up onto his lap, kissing her automatically on the forehead. She studied his face, touched his lips, and put a finger into his mouth. Her eyes were large and curious—Eleanor's eyes. She wore only a diaper—he and Eleanor called it swaddling clothes or loin cloth—and he propped her up on his thigh with his hands on her rib cage.

His son came in with a glass of apple juice. and set it down, saying, "Mom wants you to drink this. She says you can get de-hy-dre-ated on a hot day."

Edmund noticed the Lego blocks on the floor and began putting them back on the table, becoming absorbed in creating a pattern, ignoring his father and sister.

Erica wanted to get down. Clayton felt the soft sensations leave him. She crawled across the floor and sat down next to her brother, watching him intently, fascinated by the primary-colored plastic blocks that could be fitted together in so many different ways.

Eleanor came in. She was wearing shorts and her trim legs had red creases from the patio furniture. Her thick reddish-brown hair, flattened by a sun hat, was pulled back and held by an elastic band. A bandaged toe stuck out from her sandal—she had scraped it on the driveway the previous day. In her hand she held a glass of juice.

"You've got more freckles on your forehead," Clayton said tenderly.

She smiled. "You didn't drink your juice. You're going to get—"

"De-hy-dre-ated. I know. Edmund told me."

Eleanor crossed the room and looked at the drawing on the board. "So this is what all the hoo-ha's about," she said, one hand resting on Clayton's shoulder.

"Yeah, a billion-dollar hoo-ha," Clayton replied, tracing the lines in his palm with a pencil. "Just what Hartford needs, another office tower disaster. I wish the city would figure out what to do about the nightmare traffic before allowing another one of these monsters to go up."

As she glanced over the drawing, Clayton told her that it had to be finished for the clients' meeting on Monday. Eleanor asked him if he could manage it, and Clayton responded simply that he had to if he wanted to keep his job. When he said that he'd probably have to work on the weekend, Eleanor bent over to pick up Erica from the floor. Clayton wished that she would squat down when she did this. He had told her many times that bending her knees put less strain on her back, but she always picked up Erica without squatting down. At the door, Eleanor told him they were having lamb chops for dinner. "Come play with me, Dad," Edmund implored when they were alone. "I can't right now," Clayton said with annoyance and frustration. A few moments later, Edmund dashed out, slapping him on the thigh as he passed.

The moon was full that night, and its pearl-like light saturated the Simonelli house, the medieval town in miniature. Alone in the dining room after dinner, Clayton was seated at the table sipping a creme de menthe and Courvoisier from a snifter. He called his concoction Simonelli's Elixir. Cognac was usually a restorative for him. It was after 11:00. He had just finished working for the day. Eleanor and the children were in bed. His mind had been on his work, and he and Eleanor had said very little to each other during dinner.

Clayton moved to a window and looked out at the silvered trees. He saw instead a room in his family's parish church, the basement school where he and his brother and countless other grade school children had been taught to believe in mysteries, initiated into the rituals of Catholicism. A heavy crucifix hung on the plaster wall, and there was always dampness, a dank odor, and the lunar face of the nun who catechized him with the systematic questions, answers, explanations, and corrections. He did not know the questions anymore, nor the answers, certainly, but he wished he knew how to pray for the grace of God. That was something he was sure he'd need some day. Hadn't those nuns told him, he wondered, that grace was something you couldn't pray for, that redemption had to be earned? Or was it something that happened to you when you were ready for it?

The grandfather clock in the living room chimed the half-hour. Clayton's snifter was empty. He was fatigued, and he went upstairs and undressed for bed. Eleanor was awake and lay uncovered, her skin a marmoreal white. He climbed into bed and lay beside her, as still as a pharaoh in his tomb.

Rolling onto her side, Eleanor said softly, "Where are you? You've been distant all night."

"It'll pass," he replied, his voice sounding hollow.

Eleanor pressed her naked body against his. The stubble under her arm prickled his shoulder. Her fingernails pinched his genitals when she caressed them.

"I need you, baby. Make love to me," Eleanor urged. Clayton was unresponsive

"What is it? What's wrong?"

"I don't know, but I can't. I'm sorry." Clayton got out of bed in agitation. His heart was beating fast. He took the pulse in his neck. It was regular. "I don't know what's happening," he said as he started getting dressed.

Eleanor sat up. "Where are you going?" she asked in alarm.

"For a walk. I'll never get to sleep unless I take a walk. Please try to understand. It's not you. It's something in my head, but I don't know what. If this is my mid-life crisis then it's arriving a little ahead of schedule. I'll be back as soon as I can."

The air outside was cooler than it had been during the day. Clayton headed down the slope towards the river. He turned once to look back at the house. Was that Eleanor's shadow moving along the bedroom wall? He walked faster. He wasn't wearing socks, and he felt the earth through the soles of his running shoes. At the periphery of trees, he slipped into the darkness of the woods, halting to allow his eyes time to adjust. He smelled the crab apples rotting on the ground, and heard a distant chorus of frogs. The beeches and oaks were ruffled with brush. Catching sight of a flash of silver, he followed it and made his way to the river.

He had never been out here at this time of night. He found a path and took it to a clearing in the bank where he had seen men fishing. The river was dark and flowed silently. Trees leaned over in a slow motion fall. At first, the place seemed to stiffen in alarm as he entered it; he felt menaced. Then gradually it enveloped him with solitude. Sitting on a rock, Clayton looked at the smooth surface of the water and thought about the degree to which his life had changed since he had come back to

Connecticut. His fortunes had flowed very differently from what he had expected. The pace of his life was frantic. He never seemed to have enough time for anything. Hartford was becoming a little New York and commuting was a death-defying act. His brother was in California, his parents had moved to Florida, and his close friends were scattered all over the Western Hemisphere. They had come back after Eleanor's father died, so that Eleanor could be closer to her mother and their children would have a grandparent they could see more than once a year. He felt that everyone's needs had been taken into consideration except his own. In Boston, every day revitalized him. In Connecticut, it seemed to him that all he did was eat, sleep, and work. So, he thought, what is the solution, move back to Boston? That would take time, and besides, that wasn't the source of the problem. It isn't where you live, he concluded, but how you live that matters.

The next day, the air was like a steaming towel wrapped around the face of New England. In the architectural firm of Bates & Mobley, the air-conditioning went down about 11:30, and a few old fans were dug out of closets, the windows were opened, and work went on as usual. Seated at the drawing board in his office on the second floor of Bates & Mobley's renovated Victorian mansion in Hartford, Clayton switched off his Luxo lamp and continued to work by natural light. Albrecht Dürer's engraving of himself looked down from above the fireplace, a bust of Beethoven frowned in the heat, and perspiration beaded Clayton's forehead. Strange how you can't control certain body functions, he thought.

He went to the men's room and washed his face with cold water. As he was pulling back his shirt collar and rubbing a wet paper towel over his neck, one of the partners walked in. Why does this guy always catch me at an awkward moment, he wondered. Dick Mobley was a man who never seemed to sweat: his tie was straight, his hair was in place, and his shirt looked crisp. Mobley studied himself in the mirror while Clayton re-knotted his tie.

"Going to have that drawing ready for Monday, Clay?" he queried, making it sound more like an order than a question.

"No problem," Clayton returned. He noticed the file folders that Mobley usually carried when he was on his way to a meeting. "How long is this heat wave supposed to last?"

"I heard well into next week. Carrier's sending someone to work on the air. I had Stu go for more fans. You need one?"

"It's not so bad. Fans blow the papers around."

Somewhat refreshed, Clayton went back to his office, hooked his long legs on the lowest rung of the stool, and continued with the drawing. Through the open windows, he heard things he had never heard here before, since the windows were usually shut. Pigeons cooed, a man and a woman were having an argument in Spanish and Bob Dylan's "A Hard Rain's A-gonna Fall" was playing on a radio. Clayton looked out at the burnt grass of Bushnell Park, his gaze snagged by the synchronized movements of a pair of joggers. He saw himself as he was fifteen years ago, a Vietnam War protestor in a demonstration on Boston Common. Only a few nights ago, he had dreamt about Boston. He turned his attention back to the vertical black lines of the drawing and tried to concentrate. The music faded, a truck roared by, and then a siren wailed. This urban cacophony did not disturb him, but a drop of sweat that had trickled down to the end of his nose threatened the entire enterprise.

Clayton slipped the drawing from the board into a portfolio. Then he picked up his suit jacket, a copy of *The New York Times*, and a peach that he hadn't eaten after lunch. He locked his office door and left word with the receptionist. Going out into the parking lot, he felt like Dante entering a deeper circle of the Inferno. My car's probably melted, he thought; I'll find it in a pool of burgundy and silver.

The interior of his BMW smelled like cooked leather. Carefully, he placed the portfolio down flat on the back seats then climbed behind the wheel. "Damn, it's hotter than hell," he said out loud as he started the engine, turned up the air-conditioner, and drove off.

Instead of going home, however, he went to the Wadsworth Atheneum Museum on Main Street. It has been some time since I've been in there, he thought as he approached the castle-like structure with a modern wing in marble-covered granite and concrete. Before his arrival at Bates & Mobley, while he was still freelancing in Boston, he read about the competition for that wing and considered submitting a design proposal until he realized that the project would be too emotional for him. As a child, he had come here with his grandmother, a painter, to study the Italian masters; as an adolescent, he came alone to study composition or with Audrey, his first love, to share the longings of his heart and soul on Sunday afternoons, and whenever he was home from college because he was lonely and in need of spiritual healing. During the years from adolescence to his mid-thirties, when he had rejected all forms of religion, museums were the closest thing he had to a church. Walking through them—the Museum of Fine Arts, the Fogg, the Isabella-Gardner in Boston, and the Guggenheim, the Museum of Modern Art in Manhattan—he was filled with awe at the creative and visionary powers of the human imagination. It made so much more sense to him to worship in a place of creativity, the place of the muses. He had never lost faith in God, merely in organized religion, man's attempt to systematize and rationalize the mysterious and inexplicable. Whenever he was in a strange city, bookstores and museums were the places he went to feel at home, and he always met intriguing people there. It was in a museum that he first met Eleanor. He remembered the Saturday afternoon in the Fitzwilliam Museum in Cambridge when he first saw her, seated on a stool, oblivious to the throngs, sketching Delacroix's "Odalisque" with a truthfulness that stunned him. Her intense involvement in her work had been one of the most seductive things about her, and he had been unable to move on through the gallery without speaking to her. He had had that sketch matted and framed, and it was always the first thing to go up and the last to come down in their bedroom whenever they moved. That wasn't her only work on permanent exhibit. Spilling over the white hallways of the upper floor of their house were her violent and erotic art school paintings, the ones she hadn't given away. Since college, she hadn't completed a single canvas. One day she had simply stopped working, and she didn't seem to miss it. How did it happen, he wondered, that one of the most talented students in Boston hadn't lifted a paint brush in at least fifteen years? Was it because she had painted everything out of her system or because she had had children? But she had stopped working before she had had children. It was weird. This sudden loss of creativity, of the *need* to create, mystified and terrified him.

As Clayton entered the first gallery of the Wadsworth Museum, something stirred to life inside him. He felt all his frantic, scattered energy being pulled in and redirected outward with steadiness and control. He concentrated on his thoughts and feelings, focused on each canvas and flowed into its world with ease. For the first time in years he remembered he had a soul because he could feel it. So much of his daily activity was deadening: office politics and career hustling, playing the angles, manipulating for an advantage, competing for attention, making the right people happy. He hated Dick Mobley's smug superiority. How could he deal with all his bottled up rage? It was destroying him. He had neglected his soul for too long now. It had started in college, even earlier, really. He came from a family of builders. His father and grandfather built houses, and Clayton was given three choices: build them, design them, or find another family. So he had opted for architecture as a reasonable compromise that would satisfy his own creative needs as well as his father's expectations. That was fine in theory, but he wasn't doing the kind of work that fulfilled him: designing private residences. The things he designed as part of a team—office buildings and shopping malls, institutions and parking garages—had no individual personality, no soul. Nothing created by a group had any artistic value, he believed. He wanted to create as an individual. The paintings he was looking at expressed a unique vision of the world. They told the stories of the lives of their creators. He wanted to tell his own story in wood, stone, and glass, the materials of his chosen medium.

When Clayton had seen the Impressionist, Post-impressionist, Baroque, Renaissance, and Medieval paintings, he left the museum. He was in an inspired state of mind. This is the time for me to do something, he thought; this is the time for me to begin moving towards independence.

About an hour later, Clayton left Interstate 84 and made his way through Farmington. He took the roads that snaked through the smooth meadows and stony fields. This was the New England he loved, an untamed spirit, older than industry, haunted by Indian ghosts. After five years of traveling this road, he knew it as well as he knew the vein tracks on the undersides of his arms. Yet he always marveled at the piece of stone wall that ran along the road for about half a mile. This wall was to him a thing as mysterious and magical as Stonehenge or the Great Wall of China. A gray barn rotting into the earth came into view as the wall ended, and beyond this ruin was a clump of conifers, then a brook, and after that a fenced field that sloped up to a corral, stables, and a well-kept farmhouse. Clayton saw the horses in their paddock but no people. He had never seen the inhabitants of this "ranch," but knew they were New Yorkers who came for the summer. An animal darted out into the road. Clayton could not swerve fast enough, and it thumped against the front fender.

He pulled onto the shoulder, got out of the car, and walked towards the dark spot on the pavement, anxious that it might be a cat or a small dog, a raccoon or a fox. He did not want to kill any creature but especially not something beautiful. It lay on the center line, and he did not have to get any closer to see that it was an opossum, and it was unquestionably dead. He walked back to his car and drove off. Five minutes later, he turned into his driveway.

His house was the centerpiece of a park-like property encompassed by woods on three sides and bordered on the fourth by the Farmington River. He loved driving up to it. The design for the house was conceived during a pre-children vacation he and Eleanor had spent in Italy. Inspired by the hill towns of Tuscany, Clayton created a floorplan that incorporated the overall arrangement of the medieval houses clinging to their promontories. He felt this made the structure more organic, a unified whole. The house was like one of these towns in miniature. It was a house, he believed, that should have a name.

He pulled up next to Eleanor's white Cherokee jeep. No blood stained the fender, but he wanted to have the BMW washed that evening nevertheless. Entering the house through the sunroom, he saw an empty clay pot on a sheet of newspaper spread out on the tile floor, a bag of loam sitting beside it. Clayton knew immediately what this meant: Eleanor's work had been interrupted by the children. At any given moment, she had several projects in progress around the house. He admired her ability to complete them all in the course of a day. For him it was just the opposite—everything he started seemed to remain unfinished.

Clayton found Eleanor in their bedroom. She usually rested in the afternoon while the children were sleeping. The room was cool and dark. Going in, he sat by the bed and looked at her. Her oval face was serene, the skin smooth, her thin eyelids with their feathery lashes unable to keep out even the dimmest light; her lips arched prettily, her hair was a shade of red like the rooftops of Sienna, and a blue vein streaked across her left temple; the sensuous neck, curved torso, long languorous limbs—this was his wife. When someone wanted to know his favorite color he would say flesh, thinking of Eleanor's skin. Her stretched out arm, dangling her hand over the edge of the bed, trembled slightly. She stirred, sensing his presence, and opened her eyes. She looked at him for a long time without speaking. Her look disturbed him, but he managed a smile.

Apprehensively, he said, "Have I grown scales and tiny wings?"

"Today was hell for me," Eleanor said angrily. "Why didn't you call?"

"I'm sorry, El." Clayton's smile turned sheepish. "I was so damn busy I forgot."

"It isn't fair," she reproached him. "Why didn't you think of my feelings? You should have called, especially after last night."

He got up and changed his clothes, and as he did he thought of what he should say to her. Eleanor was watching him intently. He saw her eyes, full of pain, searching his back.

"If there's someone else, I want to know," she said. "I don't want to go on wondering."

So that's why she was studying my back, he thought; she was looking for scratches. "El, darling, no other woman has touched me in at least ten years," he told her tenderly, hoping his voice was steady and reassuring.

It was, but she was not affected by his tone of voice at the moment. She was too hurt. "You can't have both of us. You can have me or you can have her. But you can't have us both."

The muscles in Clayton's arms stiffened. "There is no 'her'," he said slowly and with emphasis. "Why do you assume that there's a woman involved in this?"

She was silent for a moment. "Why can't you make love to me?" she asked him with the innocence of a hurt child.

Clayton got into bed and held her. "There's no one else," he said. "Believe that." He went on to tell her that he had been working too hard, and stress was complicating the problem. He had been taking a lot of pressure from Dick Mobley over this office tower thing, which was a big deal for the firm. Mobley was driving everybody nuts over it, but especially him, since he had the most responsibility for the project. After holding each other and talking like this for a while, they felt closer. They tried to make love again, but something was still wrong. Clayton's desire was dead.

The following day was Saturday. At breakfast, Clayton told Eleanor that he was going to take the day off and finish the drawing tomorrow. Eleanor said she thought he was playing it too close, and Clayton replied that he had always thrived on playing things close.

They were having breakfast on the patio. Eleanor was seated

on a wicker love seat and Clayton was across the table from her on a folding lawn chair. The kids were playing in the yard. Clayton finished his grapefruit juice and took a bite out of a bagel. Eleanor pushed her cantaloupe wedge aside, gripped her coffee cup, and said, "Is there something wrong with me? Are you tired of me?"

"If you squeeze that cup any harder it's going to shatter."

Eleanor frowned. "Fuck the cup! Just answer me."

"It's not you," Clayton began slowly. "You are beautiful and a blessing, and as cornball as it sounds I love you more every day. It's not you. It's me." He took a deep breath. "Yesterday, I was in the Wadsworth. I used to go there when I was in high school—"

"Yes, I know," Eleanor interrupted impatiently.

Clayton looked at her. It was very important that she understand, but he didn't think she would, and in any case he didn't want to tell her unless she was in a receptive frame of mind. "This is very complicated," he said.

"You're making it complicated," Eleanor retorted. Her tone turned plaintive. "I'm in pain, Clayton. I need to know what's wrong. We've always talked things over. That's why we've survived."

Edmund threw a clump of dirt that hit Erica in the face, and she wailed with outraged dignity. Eleanor ran out to the yard and scooped her up without squatting down. There was no injury, and in a few moments Erica was comforted. Eleanor hadn't seen what had happened, and Edmund responded to his mother's questions with innocent evasiveness, offering no information that would incriminate himself. Watching them, Clayton wondered whether Eleanor was right, that he made the situation more complicated. Did he, in fact, make life more complicated than it needed to be? Life was full of contradictions and paradoxes, he thought, and nothing was simple if you were aware of them. Did Eleanor refuse to see them? Or did she find meaning in spite of them?

Clayton joined the others in the hot sunshine. He took Erica in his arms and carried her to the patio. They sat at the table and he gave her an English muffin half spread with raspberry jam. The night she was born, a jumbo jet crashed in Houston, and he had vowed never to let her get on a plane. Eleanor had not continued painting, he thought, but she had given birth to these children, and they were more important than any of the paintings he had seen.

"We've got that damned party to go to tonight," Eleanor exclaimed with annoyance. "I wish you could go without me."

"I'm not up for it either," Clayton said, "but we have to go."

It happened that they spent the rest of the day apart. Clayton took Edmund tubing on the Farmington River while Eleanor went with Erica to visit her mother in Wethersfield. They left from a recreation spot called Satan's Kingdom, drifted downriver about a mile, and were shuttled back in an old school bus. Floating along in an oversized yellow tube with Edmund clinging to his belly, Clayton was reminded of what it must be like to give birth. He remembered seeing Eleanor in that same position, her face screwed up in a grimace, he wiping the sweat from her forehead as she gripped his hand tighter than any man ever had, even while arm wrestling. Giving birth to their children, she had suffered to bring life into the world. Could he claim as much as that? Perhaps she was more attuned to the universe, could read its signs and wonders. Was the universe speaking to him, trying to guide him?

That evening, both kids went to sleep earlier than usual, and after they were in bed Clayton and Eleanor drank vodka tonics as they cleaned up the kitchen. They had another as they watched the evening news, and a third as they were getting dressed to go out to the dinner party. Clayton thought about looking back in ten years and remembering that that was the moment they became drunks because they felt trapped and could not resolve their problems.

"We're drinking too fast," Clayton said, putting down his empty glass. "We've got to pace them."

"Don't worry about it. Drunks are lucky," said Eleanor as she drained her glass and handed it to Clayton for a refill. "God looks after idiots, artists, children—and drunks."

Clayton put the glass on the dresser next to his own. "I don't want to read about us in the papers."

"The only thing worse than being talked about is not being talked about. Please make me another drink."

Clayton looked at her blouse clinging to her breasts. "Aren't you going to wear a bra with that, Oscar?"

"No . . . Why should I?"

"Your boobs are loose."

Eleanor regarded herself in the full-length mirror. "So what if my boobs are loose? You always found them appealing."

"That's the point. They're for *me* to find appealing." Clayton pulled a bra from one of her drawers and held it out to her, telling her that Dick Mobley would be there and he knew Dick Mobley was crazy about boobs.

She was holding a pump in one hand and a high heeled shoe in the other, trying to decide between them. "Is that what you talk about at the office? What naughty boys," Eleanor said, taking the bra and tossing it on the bed. "Listen, it's my body and I'll do as I damn well please with it."

"Please spare me your feminist bullshit sloganeering—"

Eleanor's well-flung shoe, the pump, struck Clayton squarely on the forehead, knocking him back on the bed. Stunned, he lay motionless, spread-eagled like a KO'd boxer. Eleanor moved frantically, loosening his tie, unbuttoning his shirt, yanking off his shoes and rubbing his feet.

"Oh, God! Oh, no! Clayton! Are you all right? Please talk to me. Say something," she pleaded, kneeling over him.

Clayton opened his eyes and smiled. "I love you," he said, caressing her face with his fingertips. "Remember the night we had a fight in the Village Gate—it was a Freddie Hubbard concert—and you threw a beer at me because of the way I was looking at the waitress? God, you are wonderful." He paused, looking up at her. "What I started to tell you yesterday," he continued, "is that I've decided to go into business for myself. I'm going to design houses, like I've always wanted to. I know it's going to take time and a lot of hard work, but it's what I was meant to do. I've already got a couple of potential clients."

Eleanor said she thought it would be very risky, that there was a lot at stake: the well-being of the family, their children's future, the house, their investments. "It's something to think about," she concluded. Clayton said he had been thinking about all of those things, and he agreed that they should work out a plan that would minimize the risks. He wouldn't leave Bates & Mobley until then. Eleanor was still skeptical, but Clayton hoped that she would eventually see it from his point of view. He did not want to lose her or the children, or their way of life, but it was insane to go on being frustrated and unfulfilled. He understood Eleanor's side of it too; she was a realist, and she feared uncertainty and anything that threatened their security. Ultimately, he believed, he had to follow his own instincts.

Arriving late for the party, Clayton and Eleanor took their seats at the dinner table in time for the salad. As they ate they endured the ribbing of their friends, smiling conspiratorially when Dick Mobley observed that they had probably stopped to go parking. Clayton went along with the joke by stating that he got the bump on his forehead when he banged it on the steering wheel while executing a position from the Kama Sutra, but he hated Mobley for the way he looked at Eleanor when she got up from the table. She was in the living room making an ice pack out of a towel and some crushed ice from the bar. It's a good thing I won't be working for that bastard much longer, he thought.

Later that night, after Clayton had taken the babysitter home, he and Eleanor made love. It had started to rain, and afterwards they talked about how the rain was a good sign. That was the last thing they said to each other before falling asleep in each other's arms. During the night, Clayton woke up and listened to the rain against the windows. Measuring the lump on his forehead between his thumb and index finger, he looked at Eleanor while she slept and watched her for a very long time. As he was going back to sleep, he thought he heard a large animal prowling on the patio. He got out of bed, went over to the window, and peered out. Through the curtains of rain, he saw a dimly lit world of half-tones and grays, but nothing unusual.

"What is it, Clay?" asked Eleanor.

"It's nothing," Clayton said as he got back into bed.

Propping herself up on one elbow, Eleanor looked at him and said, "Since you've decided to go ahead with this, there's something you should know. I've put painting aside for a while. I haven't given it up. Don't forget that I need to be creative too, and I think it's time for me to get back to my work."

He held her, hoping Eleanor meant what she said. He couldn't tell her how much he wanted her to start painting again. I have every reason to believe that God's grace has touched me—at last I have found what I believe to be my one true path, he thought as he fell blissfully asleep listening to the rain.

    It was a hard rain that kept on till morning.

The Tale of Roberto Miranda 🌲

THERE WAS ONCE a young man named Roberto Miranda who loved his family's name so much that he wanted to make it known throughout the world. Since he had no artistic talent, business skill, or athletic prowess, he decided he would discover a new place and he dreamt of seeing "Miranda Mountain" or "River Miranda" or the "Isle of Miranda" on a map and hearing people talk about it as if it had had that name from the beginning of time. "I'm going to make you proud to be a Miranda," he told his wife and children. So one day in September he said goodbye to his wife and two children in their little blue house by a ravine in New Hampshire and set out for the rest of the world. Traveling by boat, train, camel, and horseback, Roberto journeyed from continent to continent, from the Andes to Katmandu, from Malaysia to Tasmania from Yosemite to the Yukon seeking the undiscovered terrain that would be grand enough to bear his family's name and make it famous throughout the world. But no matter how far he traveled, no matter how wild or remote the territory Roberto found that it had already been discovered—it already had a name. The years went by and Roberto became a middle-aged man but still the unnamed place he sought eluded him. At last Roberto wanted to go home. He made his way by freighter across Hudson Bay in Canada, rode in a box car through Quebec and so came back to New Hampshire, a haggard, worn out man with yellow teeth, a gray beard and glassy, yellowish eyes. The little blue house still stood by the ravine but other people lived there now, two divorced women roommates; they had made many improvements, including a garden, a gazebo and a high fence along the ravine. "Can you tell me what happened to my family? They used to live here," Roberto croaked when one of the women opened the door a little. The other woman came out and the two of them looked at each other and then at Roberto. "Oh, the Miranda family," one of them said. "A sad story. The husband disappeared one day, some say with another woman, and eventually his wife went mad and threw herself into Miranda's Ravine." "And the children?" Roberto stammered. "What happened to the children?" The other woman told him they had changed their names and moved away. Roberto set out again in search of his children. The months went by and then the years but Roberto never found them. He was sleeping in a box car when the sound of two men talking awoke him. "Just take the road that goes out to Miranda's Ravine," one of the men said. "The place where that woman killed herself." Roberto closed his eyes again, a smile pulling at his lips. And then he died.

The Carpenter's Son ⚜

JOE GAMBINO STOOD at a window in the upstairs quarters of the Society of St. Anthony, a glass of beer in one hand, and took in the warm, red August evening on Endicott Street. What he saw pleased him, the bustle and the noise it produced had a pattern and a familiarity that satisfied something in him. Splaying open the Venetian blind to the full spread of his coarse carpenter's hand, he could see across the street the sultry tenements of red brick which had baked in the sun all day long, their cluttered outline against the rose-tinted sky, their well-kept porches where the old women in black were sitting tending their bambini and gossiping while the older children made mischief on the sidewalk. All of this satisfied him. It reminded him of Padua and his childhood, but it was also the community he had helped to build. Birds twittered and sang their twilight songs, pigeons cooed in the eaves, people stood talking in clusters all along the street, and the shopkeepers were closing up early. Theo Paletti, who kept the corner grocery store, was shooing away the children who were stealing his strawberries.

It was a Friday in August, 1962; tomorrow would be the 55th Grand Religious Festival of St. Anthony of Padua Da Montefalcione, and further up the street the statue of St. Anthony reposed in a red, pink and gold sidewalk chapel. Even from this distance, Joe recognized the people who stood in line, awaiting a turn to attach a dollar bill to the streamers that flowed down from the saint like those on the ship that had taken him and his wife across the Atlantic to America. They were his neighbors, his friends and his business associates. The men wore overalls, one carried a tray of wrenches, that was Frank Mendetto, the plumber, another was resting one foot on an enormous box of tools, Auggie Luciano, the electrician, and others. He knew the name and the trade of them all. The women were dressed in faded cotton and black shawls. Their names he knew as well, their husbands' income, where they lived, where they were born and the number of children in the family. The names of the children and those of the old people were more difficult, and Joe was always mixing them up, much to their amusement. After all, he said, he was a carpenter not the priest who baptized them. These were his people, he was intimately acquainted with their lives and fortunes, as they were with his and his family's and together they comprised the Italian community in the North End of Boston.

After Joe had fed his eyes long and contentedly on the scene in the street, he released the blind with a snap, turned around and finished off his beer in one satisfying swallow. The clubroom of the Society was beginning to fill up as more and more of the men left off working early and headed for home by way of the club. Joe greeted each of the newcomers heartily across the room, his swarthy arms folded proudly over his chest, his heavy boots planted apart, he stood like a bull caribou overlooking his bucks.

"Come sit down, Joe. Have another beer," entreated a fat, red-faced man named Carmen whose face was kept flushed by the heat of his restaurant.

"No, thanks," Joe politely declined, filling his pockets with his hands. He did not like Carmen, but as president of the Society he was obliged to treat everyone with courtesy.

The room was full of men now, all familiar and easy with one another, and the conversation started to boil like broth in a cauldron. The fire under the cauldron was beer, nobody drank anything else except on special occasions like the Festival when the Society provided brandy and wine, and the meat in the broth was the subject of the Festival and the money it would raise.

Joe wet a cigar between his lips, bit off the end, lit it with a wooden match and puffed luxuriously at it for several moments while he listened intently to the comments and differences of opinion which shot back and forth across the room. Joe's stature was small, but it commanded authority. The conversations subsided almost immed-iately and in the dramatic pause, while all eyes were fixed on him, Joe puffed theatrically on his cigar.

"Fellow members of the Society of Saint Anthony," he said with gravity, "I have come to a decision in regard to the money we will collect from this year's Festival and how it should be spent." The silence in the room was flawless and all eyes were focused with surprised expectancy upon Joe. "It has been the practice of the Society in the past to donate the money to charity or some worthy cause, such as the year we helped to buy a kidney machine for the hospital—"

"And the athletic equipment for the high school," interrupted Dom Morreale the truck driver, a big-shouldered, long-armed hulk of a man with skin like leather and a bald head, whose son was captain of the football team. Everyone laughed, Dom's pride in his son was well known.

"And the year we bought athletic equipment for the high school," Joe repeated unperturbed, smiling fondly at the big, dim-witted man. Then the smile faded and his face became dour. He had waited a long time for this moment. "I propose that the money we collect this year be used to finance my political campaign."

The men were stunned by this announcement, their faces went blank as fish. Joe tensed up inside, prepared to withstand the wave of the men's resistance when it came. He did not embrace their stares directly but looked slightly above their heads like an experienced actor. Frank and Auggie came in, put down their tools and stood with confusion written all over their faces against the wall near the full-length reproduction of St. Anthony holding the baby Jesus. The rush of the wave came, most of the men expressed their opposition and anger, but there was no undertow to pull him down.

"My campaign," Joe shouted, the hand which held the cigar raised to quell the gibbering objections, "My campaign, Gentlemen," he repeated in his normal volume, "for a seat on the City Council."

The broth fairly erupted out of the cauldron.

Carmen struggled to sit up from the deep cushions of the sofa, his fat arms bulging out of his shirt sleeves. "We don't want any part of no politics, Joe Gambino," he burst out, breathless.

Many others fired off their agreement to this.

"This is no place for politics," somebody said.

"We'll have the boys with the limousines comin' here next."

Joe puffed on his cigar, sure of his superiority. With a shrewdness that recommended his political abilities he did not attempt to shout anyone down but waited, calmly and confidently, for his self-assured silence to defeat the onslaught of opinion. Embarrassed by their outburst in the face of Joe's quiet self-control, the other men at length surrendered the floor and awaited the inevitable speech by their elected president.

"Now, my brothers of the Society of Saint Anthony, let me give it to you straight. As you are all aware, this society was founded by us for two very important reasons. The Society was organized first and foremost to bring over friends and relatives from the old country, provide them with food, clothes and a place to live until they can get on their feet, help the husband find work and assist them every step of the way in becoming naturalized citizens of the United States of America. The necessity for these services is obvious to all of us since we have all been through it at one time or another, and of course most of our money goes to help *il immigrante*. The second purpose of our club is to protect the rights of the Italian people of our community. In the past we have donated money to the Italian hospital, the Italian schools and the Catholic church, we have paid lawyers' fees, doctor bills and even bribed a few policemen with the money collected in the name of our patron saint, all for the good of some Italian who was down on his luck. Have we ever refused anyone who came to us for help?" Several pairs of eyes were cast down at this question. "But I put it to you, friends, what real good does it do? How many of you run the risk of finding yourselves down on your luck all over again, eh? *Capisce? Fratelli*, I ask you, is it always *malo fortuna* or is it sometimes maybe politics that takes a man's job away or pays him only this much when he needs that much to live a decent life? You yourselves know what it can mean to know the right person, to have a fratello in government, it is good, no? Si, si, si, you're damn right it is good, how do you think the Irish got so much, eh? Politics. Yeah, sure, we live our own lives here, we don't mix too much with the others, but how long can we live with our head up our ass, eh, how long? We all pay taxes, don't we, where do you think the money goes, not into our North End, that's for damn sure, it goes into some Irish's pocket in City Hall or into some Irish's new house. How long you want to go on making life more comfortable for some Irish's kid, eh, how long? And some of us need special licenses to run our business, some of us need special contracts with the government, that takes *influence, fratelli, influenza* and contacts with the right people in that big building on Tremont Street. With *influenza* you get good contracts and good contracts means good money. You, Auggie, you want to fix toilets all your life or you want to have a nice business with men workin' for you and lots of government money?" Auggie grinned like a spaniel and would have wagged his tail obediently if he had had one. "Of course you want good money and a good job, we all do. That's why we came to this country in the first place. Some of us were starving in the old country, but here life is better for all of us. We all miss the places where we were born, bella Italia, but we must not forget our children and how much better off they will be. This country's got so much money it's gonna sink and most of it is in the pockets of a few big families like the Rockefellers and the Kennedys. Why shouldn't we get our share of the pie? Inflation don't mean nothing. How long you want to work like dogs for snotty Irish kids, eh, how long before we smarten up and learn we gotta protect ourselves in government?"

The men looked sheepishly at one another. This traditionally male sanctuary was infiltrated through the open windows by the sound of their wives' voices on Endicott Street calling their children home to supper. Joe's stare measured the resistance in the eyes of the key men in the room. There was none.

"Wait a minute, Joe, how you gonna get me a liquor license?"

challenged Theo Paletti, the owner of the corner grocery store.

"With the right influence, answered Joe confidently, "it'll be as easy as asking Father Marchetti for a blessing."

Everyone laughed loudly. Father Marchetti had a habit of blessing everyone he met. "That's old Joe, always fast with a joke."

"Now, if there are no more questions, I move that we take a vote—"

"I have a question."

Alberto Sorenna, the eldest son of Vittorio Sorenna, a waiter in an elegant Newbury Street restaurant, and the only one of their sons to have spent some time in university, raised his hand. He had returned to the North End in search of his ethnic roots and became the youngest member of the Society.

"What makes you think that you won't become like the Irish . . . We need a man who cares for his people . . . What makes you a better man for the job than—"

Alberto didn't have a chance to finish his sentence before Vittorio leaped up and slapped him hard across the face. "Don't you talk to Joe Gambino that way! I'll kill you! I don't care if you are my son. I'm ashamed of you. Who the hell are you to talk about caring for your people, you with your college big-shot ideas. I'm sorry, Joe."

"Leave the boy alone, Vittorio. He's one of this new generation of smartasses blaming the older generation for all the wrong in the world. But they'll learn when it's their turn to run the country, they'll learn not to bite the hand that feeds them."

"We won't make such a mess of it, that's for damn sure—"

Vittorio slapped him again. "You shut up now. I told you I'll kill you and I mean it!"

"Since you asked me, Alberto, I'll tell you why I won't become like the Irish. Because I believe in God, that's why. Not your Irish go-to-church-on-Sunday kind of god, but a real God who gets angry and kicks you in the balls for cheating him or lyin' to him. The god of the Irish is a sissy next to my God. My God means what he says, I can't be a two-faced hypocrite like them, and what my God says scares the shit out of me . . .

"Now, let's take a vote."

As the men were raising their hands to vote, Joe's son Antonio was sitting with his girlfriend, Maryellen, on the edge of the Copley Square fountain beneath the imposing Victorian frown of Trinity Church. Like the modern Square, they were young and contradictory against the Victorian architecture of the city. Their school books were cast beside them. The evening was warm and bright. Crowds hurried home from work along Boylston Street, old people fed pigeons. Antonio, lean and tall, had red lips and large brown eyes that were infatuated with Maryellen, who was a beauty, an Irish beauty. She was fiery and vigorous, full of life, her green eyes coruscated like the cool green water of the fountain and her cheeks were warm and blushing like peaches in the sun.

Maryellen was his first love, and he secretly adored her. They walked together after school until supper time, when Antonio walked her home to the edge of Clancy Street. She never allowed him to go further, to walk her to her door, because her family disliked Italians ever since leaving the North End and her brothers were big and fierce.

"You're so different from my brothers and their friends," Maryellen complained. "They are loud and clumsy, but at least they have fun. Why can't you enjoy things more, Antonio? Why do you always look so sad? My friends have noticed."

Antonio felt the blood rising to his cheeks. He hated to be compared to her brothers and he didn't care in the least about her friends.

"How long have we been seeing each other now, nearly a month, I guess, and I've never seen you look happy. Not once. Why can't we have more fun."

Antonio shrugged. He didn't care much. By way of reply, he leaned nearer and kissed her soft, timid lips. "That's what makes me happy," he teased.

Her cheeks flamed red hot. "I don't like kissing, especially in public," she reprimanded. "Besides, someone might see us and tell my parents about you."

He dangled his hand in the water, playing with the ripples.

"Let them. It's about time they knew."

Maryellen stood up and bent over for her books. Antonio could see the silky skin and delicate hairs of her back where the shirt was stretched out of her jeans. He was also favored with a glimpse of white underthings.

"When you start talking like that it makes me wonder if you really are a trustworthy person. I expect you to have some consideration for my feelings. Is that too much to ask?"

She started away.

"Where are you going?"

Maryellen didn't answer.

Antonio grabbed his books and went after her. She turned around.

"No, Antonio, I'm going to walk home alone. I'm afraid you might do something that'll embarrass me, and I could never forgive you for that."

Antonio stood still and watched her go. She was like a wild animal that needs nothing from outside its own element. He turned and walked slowly away.

Joe walked home with Carlo and Roberto, the oldest members

of the Society and both Montys, men from Montefalcione. In the beginning, in the 'forties and 'fifties, an immigrant had to be a Monty in order to get into the club, but a lot had changed in twenty years, and Dominic Facci had even gone so far as to suggest that they take in some of the Irish who remained in the community because they were unable to follow their brethren's footsteps into the respectable lower-middle-class enclave of South Boston, but Joe and his elder officers had vetoed the idea. They knew the Irish who stayed did so out of necessity, not loyalty, and that they would jump at the first opportunity to become Southies. The man who made the proposal was married to one of the Irishmen's daughters, and he was never trusted again.

At the corner, Joe said good-bye to the old men and turned towards home. His senses registered but his mind ignored the rich aromas of tomato sauce and eggplant, garlic and chicken which wafted out of open windows, it was spinning fast like the wheels on the donkey carts back home. So far he had been able to keep the big boys with the black limousines out of his neighborhood; business was clean, but he couldn't say how long it would stay clean. Politics was not a clean business. It was a crazy world, a crazy country, and Joe had to do the best he could to help his family and his friends survive until . . . until what?

Ginette was cutting bread when he came in. A hard-working, dignified little woman, she stood at the counter, holding and slicing the loaf with large, sure hands. She toiled in her kitchen as naturally as a bee in a hive, the bluish gas in the burners licked at steaming pots, and she kept a vigilant eye on the two girls who were setting the table. Her black hair was hidden under a kerchief and thereby kept out of the food.

Joe stripped off his work jacket and shirt and hung them

behind the cellar door. His arms were sinewy and powerful, brown past the elbows and flour-white at the shoulders. He made a mental note to purchase a suit, white shirts and ties.

"You're late. The macaroni's started to stick."

Joe teased his wife's fretful temper by giving her loud, playful kisses on the cheek. Then he hugged and kissed his two bright-eyed, long-haired daughters who were sitting at the kitchen table giggling at their father's tipsy clowning.

"Maybe for you work is forgotten when you walk in the door, but not for me. Why're you smiling like Punchinello?" Ginette said in Italian. They spoke Italian with each other and English with the children.

"Because I love my family."

"And you love your beer with the boys at the Club. Here, make the salad dressing, but go easy, the price of olive oil is up fifty cents."

Joe performed this ritual task deftly, measuring out the oil and vinegar instinctively, mixing the salad with his rough hands. Then he sat down in his usual place at the head of the table.

"Where's Antonio?"

Ginette set the bowl of macaroni on the table with eyes averted. "Let Papa take his first, girls, so he can take most of the sauce off the top," she said in English.

"I said where's Antonio."

Ginette was back at the counter, filling yet another bowl with meatballs and sausages. "He hasn't come home yet, that's where he is."

Joe detected some secrecy between his wife and his son and his incendiary temper caught fire. He stood up. The kitchen floor shook under his heavy work boots as he raged into the living room, threw open the front door, and gave a sharp, commanding whistle.

Antonio was walking up Endicott Street in the sunset. The sound of his father's piercing whistle made the hair on the back of his neck stand up. At the same moment he saw his father standing in the doorway of their house on the top of the hill in his undershirt. How embarrassing, to be whistled for like a dog by his father, a man who stood on the front steps in his T-shirt with his pot belly sticking out for all the neighborhood to see. He blushed with shame for himself and his father. If his Irish friends saw him now how they would laugh, and tease and punch him. If Maryellen could see him now! His father whistled again and looked up the street in the opposite direction. Antonio ran back down the hill and ducked into an alley, panting with excitement, thinking how easy it is to deceive grown ups.

He knew he was going to catch hell from his father when he got home, and probably a slap across the head, too, but he was too proud to be treated like a dog, refusing to obey a whistle. He was enjoying this new feeling of freedom born of defiance and self-assertion. There was another whistle, and then another. His will faltered. If he went back now, then maybe . . . but no, he was too stubborn. He dreaded his father's temper, but he dreaded more the part he would have to play in tomorrow's Festival. For the last ten years, since he was five, he had had to take part in the Festival, and every year it had been the same, he had carried that stupid flag of Montefalcione at the head of the procession while all year long the statue of St. Anthony was kept in a special cupboard in his bedroom.

But this year he wouldn't do it. Anger welled up in him quickly, for he had inherited his father's temper, and tears started to his eyes. Patty and Michael had threatened to be there, and he knew what that meant, a big joke at his expense. Then they would tell Maryellen and make him look the fool. Why did his father make him do these things. Didn't he know that the Festival meant nothing to him, humiliated him? Why couldn't he be more dignified and unemotional like his friends' fathers. They didn't whistle for their sons out the front door in their T-shirts, and they didn't run after them down the street as his father had done once, shouting in Italian. It was humiliating the way his family and all the other families on Endicott Street had to do everything out in the open, the way they exposed their hearts. And he couldn't help it either, this exposing of his heart, and he hated himself for it.

His father's whistling had stopped. The street was quiet, all the children were eating their suppers.

"I won't go home," Antonio vowed out loud, picking up a rock and flinging it against the brick wall, "I won't be in their stupid festival."

He stepped out of the alley and looked up and down the street. It was empty. Shoving his hands decisively into his pockets, he set off with long strides back the way he had come.

Joe's supper had gone cold, he hadn't touched it. He sat sullenly at the table, smoking a cigar. The girls had eaten half of what was on their plates and gone into the living room to watch television. For some inexplicable reason, they shared the guilt with their brother.

Ginette was clearing away the dishes and they clattered into the sink, setting Joe's nerves on edge. She covered the two untouched meals with a dishtowel, "la moppina," and placed them in the oven to keep warm.

Joe moved to the back door and flicked his cigar defiantly out onto the driveway. "Who does he think he is, not coming home for supper. I'll beat the living daylights out of him if he's up to some trick. He can't play rebel with me."

"He's just out late with his friends, that's all."

"What friends, I never see him around this neighborhood any more. Where does he go to play with his friends?"

Ginette began the washing up, paying Joe as little attention as possible. "Don't shout at me like that. He goes downtown sometimes."

"Downtown? You let him go downtown? God knows what he's getting into down there, or who he's hanging around with."

"I don't let him, Giuseppe, he just goes."

Joe put on his shirt, let down his pants and tucked it in. Then he took his jacket from the hook on the cellar door and flung it over his shoulder. "Just tell him to keep his ass in here all night when he comes home because I want to talk to him. I'll kill him if he tries to pull some stunt tomorrow."

"Where're you going now?"

The screen door slammed shut as Joe shouted back over his shoulder, "Where do you think. I'll call you later."

Ginette turned off the tap and put her red hands into the steamy, soapy water.

There were only two other members in the Club when Joe arrived, Vittorio Sorenna and his son Alberto, the university drop-out. They were sitting on the sofa playing checkers. Joe went to the refrigerator behind the bar and got himself a beer. The bottle-opener was hanging from a string and the top fell to the floor.

"Hey, Joe," Vittorio called, "Alberto says he saw your kid walking down Endicott."

Joe took a slow swallow of beer, feigning indifference. "Oh yeah? So what."

"I gave him a ride," Alberto said snidely.

"That makes you a big man to chauffeur my kid around town. Where'd ya take him?"

"Clancy Street."

Joe froze with the beer bottle half-way to his lips, his eyes lancing shafts of hatred across the room at his young and bearded rival, then he tipped it back and finished it off in one swallow, dropped the bottle on the counter and rushed out.

His black Chevrolet was parked outside. Joe jumped in and the engine roared instantly. With tires squealing in a cloud of blue smoke he sped up the hill. The car lunged onto the expressway, swerved in and out of the traffic, and in less than fifteen minutes he was on Clancy Street, the street where stores have shamrocks in the windows. During his stint as a cab driver he had never crossed the city in such good time.

The sun had sunk behind the lowest houses and the light was fading fast. Joe nearly ran down his own son. Antonio was sitting on the curb, his head between his knees, spitting blood. He only looked up when he recognized his father's work boots. All of Joe's anger melted into compassion when he saw Antonio's face. One eye was swollen and black, and his lip was split, the blood ran from his nose. He had taken quite a beating.

Without a word, Joe helped his son into the car. Antonio turned his face shamefully away from his father's eyes. Sitting in the front seat beside him, he kept his head down and averted. He would rather have looked into the faces of strangers than his father's face. Joe pulled out his big white handkerchief and threw it into Antonio's lap.

"Who did this to you." Joe accelerated around the corner and the tires squealed in complaint. He wanted to be out of the neighborhood as quickly as possible.

Antonio maintained an obstinate and defiant silence.

His son's habitual sulking infuriated Joe, and he blamed his wife for giving in to the boy too often. She had a soft heart. "I said who did this to you," Joe shouted.

Antonio remained silent. He was afraid of his father, and he knew he would have to avoid making any explanations because he would be beaten all over again if he told his father his reason for going to Clancy Street. But he realized he must say something to keep his father from losing his temper. At last he said, "Some bigger guys. They were teasing me."

"Irish?"

"I don't know."

With alarming suddenness, Joe swung the car to the side of the road and slammed on the brakes. Antonio's face was full of fear and panic, he looked as if he would jump from the car and run for his life. The fear in his son's eyes caused a forgotten experience to flash across Joe's memory: it was in Padua, when he was twelve, and his father was beating him in the street with a stick.

Joe picked up his unused handkerchief and started to wipe the blood from Antonio's nose and mouth. There was kindness and compassion in his voice when he spoke.

"I don't want to know why you ran away from me when I called you. I don't want to know what you were doing on Clancy Street. But answer me this, why do you treat your family worse than you'd treat a dog? Is it because we've loved you? Is it because we've fed you and protected you all these years? Is it because we only want the best for you?"

The headlights from passing cars swept over his father's face, making him seem old and sad. Horns honked as the cars thundered past. Antonio was embarrassed by this unprecedented display of affection. It confused him and robbed him of all his adolescent fury and pride. But there was stubbornness in him still.

"I don't want to be in the Festival tomorrow."

Joe pulled his hand away so quickly that it made Antonio's head jerk back and strike the window frame.

"You want to humiliate me in front of all my friends! I'll kick you outta the house for this! Don't think you can play the rebel with me."

"All right."

"All right what, smart guy."

"I'll leave tonight. Right now, if you want me to."

Joe raised his arm to strike his son with a powerful backhand blow, but he hesitated. Looking at the defiant face with its black eye and bloody lip, he couldn't do it. Its stubbornness and pride arrested him.

"All right nothing. Just where in hell d'ya think you're going?"

"I'll go somewhere," Antonio replied courageously.

Joe stared straight ahead at the speeding traffic. He counted on his son being home for breakfast, one night alone in the city would be enough to break his rebellious spirit. "Get out," he said.

Antonio got hurriedly out and slammed the door. The familiar car sped off and was quickly lost in traffic. He was shaking so much he could hardly climb over the cables, and he fell several times going down the embankment.

Early in the afternoon of the next day, in the hot sunshine, the statue of St. Anthony was lifted gently from the sidewalk chapel and raised onto the shoulders of Antonio's father and five other men. Alberto Sorenna hoisted up the flag of Montefalcione, its colors unfurling in the sun. The spectators massed along both sides of Endicott Street were cheering as the Saint began his procession through the North End preceded by the brass band led by Antonio's uncle Marco. Marching behind the Saint his two sisters were among the little girls in white dresses carrying violets and chrysanthemums, and behind them were the old women with candles and rosary beads, Antonio's grandmother

among them, the thankful devotees to the saint who had granted
the petitions of their prayers. The procession moved slowly and
joyfully up Endicott Street, the red, green and white banners and
flags swaying proudly and rejoicefully high over the heads of all.
The spectators amassed in the street and marched slowly after.

Antonio watched the procession from the second floor of his
grandmother's house until the crowd had turned the corner and
the last of the stragglers, the young boys and the dogs, were out
of sight. Although he could no longer see the procession, he
knew every step and every ceremony of the route by heart, and
he stood in his underwear looking into the eerily empty street
and listening to the far-away notes of the trumpets and
trombones. The Saint would stop at individual homes where he
would be given banners of money, some lowered from windows
on ribbons, and at other windows a mother would hold out her
child to kiss his face and place a wreath of dollar bills over his
head. Confetti would fall like the first winter snow and the old
men would shout "Italia! Italia mia!" and "Italia nella esilia!" and
"Vive Italia!" with tears in their eyes. There would be tears in
the old people's eyes, in his mother's eyes, and his father's too.

If Patty and Michael came to laugh at him, they would be
disappointed. The way he was feeling right now, proud and
ashamed, he didn't care if he ever saw them again in his life, and
he wouldn't ever see them again unless they came to call for him
in *his* neighborhood. He would never be able to see Maryellen
again. Her brothers would tell her what fun they had had
beating him up.

The procession will continue until three o'clock when it will
reach the platform in the park where his sister, dressed as an
angel, will be lowered down by ropes and where his father will
make his annual speech full of gratitude and promises above the
red, green and white bunting. Then the long tables will be

spread with macaroni and homemade cookies, cheeses, cold cuts, bread, fruits and nuts. Then there will be dancing and eating, drinking and celebration while the sun set and long after the lanterns were lit. Maybe he would go out later on if he were feeling better. Right now he felt much too tired; he had been up most of the night. He lay down. The cool pillowcase soothed his sore eye. The streets were completely still except for the occasional barking of dogs. He could hear the ticking of the big old clock in the dining room. How good it was to lie in bed listening to these familiar sounds.

His grandmother was kind to him. She had scolded him for waking her up so late, but she hadn't thought twice about taking him in and nursing his eye and lip. In the morning she made him a big, delicious breakfast and while he was eating it, he listened to her speaking softly in Italian over the telephone to his mother and then to his father. She will make the peace between us, he thought. Then he would speak to him about helping to carry the statue next year, when his father would be an important man on the city council as his grandmother had told him he would be. Gazing upon the old-fashioned, sun-filled room, he closed his eyes and fell peacefully asleep.

The Things of This World ✦

TWO MONKS WERE walking through the Tuscan hills in May 1932 when they came to a ridge overlooking a pool of deep blue water glistening in the sunlight. Upon the surface of the pool floated a dark-haired maiden in blissful oblivion. The first monk, who was tall and youthful, halted and gazed down from the high embankment.

"Why have you stopped? Surely we haven't reached the monastery yet," queried the second monk who was half-blind, short and stocky with graying temples and a reddish bristle on his cheeks.

"I have paused to admire the glories of the sunset," intoned Emilio, a slender youth of nineteen, as he continued to gaze with fascination upon the naked body of the young woman.

The older monk, whose name was Dominic, examined the younger man's face closely and saw the anguish in his large brown eyes. "It is sinful to look with too much desire upon the things of this world," he declared.

"That may be, Brother Dominic, but they are so lovely. It is terribly hard to ignore them when you love them as much as I do."

"Think upon eternity and not upon the merely temporal. The things of this world are passing . . . Let us go," he snapped. "We will be late for vespers."

Reluctantly, Brother Emilio turned away and plodded along the path to the monastery in front of Brother Dominic, making the rest of the journey in silent contemplation.

After a restless night Brother Emilio left the monastery before the sun had risen. When he had gone a mile or so he stole a mule and a change of clothes from a farmyard and then continued on his way to the local village. After several hours of random inquiries he learned that a band of gypsies was encamped in the nearby hills. He made his way there on his stolen mule and by midday laid eyes on the raven-haired beauty he had beheld on the previous day.

"I need to speak with you," Emilio told her. "I saw you bathing in the river yesterday at sunset."

The beautiful young woman saw the intense desire and anguish in his large brown eyes. "So you were one of the monks standing on the ridge.

Emilio's face reddened. "I cannot deny it. I have decided to leave the monastery for good. I can keep my vows no longer. I wish to marry you."

Having found the monk handsome, well spoken and highly appealing the woman smiled invitingly. "You must speak with my father," she said, lowering her eyelids and looking down shyly. "But he is a hard man who will ask a high price for his only daughter."

Emilio spoke with the woman's father, a taciturn, big-shouldered man, and that night agreed to his terms. In exchange for his daughter the poor Emilio would allow the gypsies access to the monastery where they could help themselves to the treasures hidden away in its vaults and crypts. He returned and later that night let them in through the kitchen door. The gypsy robbers took as much gold and silver as they could carry and disappeared into the hills. Emilio caught up with them and within a week had married beautiful Ayanna in a joyous gypsy ceremony.

Seven years later, in southern Italy, Emilio's beautiful wife was bitten by a tarantula and died at the age of twenty-three. A few months later his two children were kidnapped by bandits who also stole all of his worldly possessions.

Within a week Emilio had returned to his old monastery in the northern part of the country. Brother Dominic, now the Abbot, stockier and his hair completely gone, looked upon him through his thick spectacles and saw a deeper anguish in his large eyes.

"I have come back," Emilio said, "and I am ready to relinquish the things of this world if you will teach me how."

Seeing that the younger man's soul was in torment, Friar Dominic took pity on him and granted him a second chance.

Brother Emilio proved himself to be a rehabilitated and pious monk for the first year. Then, one August day while working in the vineyard, he overheard two mezzardi, or migrant workers, talking about a band of gypsies encamped in the hills and commenting on the orphan children who could only be his own. That evening he borrowed a horse, rode into the hills, and found the gypsy camp in the same location as when he first encountered them. His two children were indeed among them, in the care of their grandfather, a sharp-eyed old man who now drove an even harder bargain.

"I ransomed them myself," he barked, "and gave them to my

son. Go back to your monastery, little monk. You are not fit to be a gypsy father." And he spat upon the ground in a demonstration of his ultimate contempt.

"Please, just let me see them. I beg you," Emilio pleaded.

The hardened old man pulled out his dagger for reply as a line of men formed on either side of him.

Seeing that he had no chance of winning back his children, Emilio started to leave only to discover that his horse had vanished. He trudged back to the monastery on foot and arrived the next morning, at Matins. By now the entire monastery knew about his gypsy offspring. The Abbot was surprised to see him. With what remained of his compassion he permitted Emilio to spend one more morning at the monastery. Emilio bathed, prayed, and cleaned out his tiny room.

Later that day, with his worldly possessions packed in a small suitcase, the disgraced monk arrived by bus in Rome. Luckily, he found immediate employment as a dishwasher in a convent school. Gradually, he worked his way up to cook. He spent more than three years slaving for the sisters who ran the elementary school, saving almost every lira he could spare from his meager salary, and praying daily for forgiveness. His heart was deeply contrite, and he begged God to accept his daily acts of repentance for all the hurtful and selfish things he had done.

When he had been at the convent school for almost four years, the mother superior shocked Emilio by putting him in charge of an orphanage in America. Emilio accepted the assignment with boundless gratitude and boarded the steamship for New York with a full heart and eyes brimming with tears.

He proved to be a wise choice. He adjusted rapidly to life in New York City and ran his orphanage on the Lower East Side with brilliance and compassion. Emilio loved his parentless brood as if they were his own children. Emilio turned out to be a gifted spokesman with a genius for raising donations. Whenever he spoke at a fundraising dinner he would end his speech by fervently intoning, "Someone must care for and love the children. They are, after all, the most precious things of this world." The audience was always deeply moved.

Adriana's Eyes ⚜

I.

AN AMERICAN WOMAN named Adriana DeSalvo was very beautiful in the classical style that was the ideal of the 1940's: she was tall, her eyes were big and dark, and her hair was long and black. She came from a refined Calabrian family and grew up expecting the best of everything. She married into a rich Italian-American family at the age of twenty-one, thinking she was set for life, but then her husband's father got sick and the family fortune drained away, and when he died in 1953 he left his home to his wife and the family business to his oldest son, Adriana's husband. That was the beginning of Adriana's misfortunes.

Adriana's husband was a handsome man with a kind heart but he loved to play the horses more than anything in the world and went to the race track at least twice a week even though Adriana begged him not to bring the family to ruin and his four children stood beside their mother with sadness in their eyes as they watched him walk silently out the door. The family business suffered even more, and they began living from hand to mouth, despite the fact that it was America's most prosperous decade. "It is hard to keep our dignity without enough money," Adriana would tell her husband. "My clothes are beginning to look shabby and your daughters have only one good dress between them. Are you a man? What do you intend to do about it? Cappercato! Soon we will have to hide our heads in shame." And the children would gather around their beautiful mama and look up at their father with big melancholy eyes but that would never stop him from taking his gambling hat from the rack and walking out the door. Yet the children were always glad when he came home; they loved their father, he was playful and funny, though they knew he could get along very well without them. Although he was kind to them and never said a harsh word, sometimes resentment would flash in his eyes and the children knew as children do that he really cared very little for them, and there were undeniable moments when they saw this truth in each other's eyes.

So it went for many years with the father running the clothing business into the ground and going off to the race track whenever he could. Adriana kept the accounts for the retail men's store, nothing financial was hidden from her, but she never learned the details of her husband's gambling. He was very secretive about his "system" for keeping track of his winnings and losses, saying nothing at all unless he was asked directly and always responding vaguely to Adriana's sardonic "And how did Diamond Giacomo make out this time?" with a "Not too bad," and if pressed insisting it would be better not to talk about it in front of the children.

The children grew up believing in their father's shame,

hearing their mother speak openly of it to friends and family alike, and praying with her for their father's salvation and their own deliverance from the poverty that dominated their lives.

One of the boys was especially sensitive to this family strife. This was Julian, the younger of the two sons. More than the others, he was torn between his love for both parents. He wanted to please both, to make both of them happy, wanted to heal the rift between them. He wanted his father to stop gambling so his mother would be happy and he wanted his mother to let his father do exactly what he liked so his father would be happy too.

"Why don't you want him to play horses, Mama?" he had asked in his ten-year-old innocence, his big brown eyes watching her.

"Because his gambling will ruin us. It will put us on the street without a roof over our heads. It will turn us into beggars," she declared excitedly.

"But why doesn't he win more money, Mama?"

"Because he's unlucky, I suppose. That's just the way it is. If God wanted him to win he would win. But what God doesn't wish can't happen, only your father won't accept that. He's unlucky. That's his fate, and it will never be any different I'm afraid."

"Does fate come from God?" asked the boy, looking up into his mother's eyes.

"Yes, I guess you could put it that way."

"Then I will ask God to change papa's fate and make him lucky," the boy said simply, his eyes full of courage and conviction as he knelt down to pray.

"I hope He listens to you, but God does as he pleases," replied the mother with a strange laugh.

A few years later the father disappeared from their lives. The business was lost—they were forced into bankruptcy. The older son had joined the marines and had been sent to Vietnam. The woman would have to go to work to support herself and her three remaining children.

"Let me go to work," the boy declared with fervor. "I will support you, Mama."

"You! You're only twelve years old!" she laughed. "But I do appreciate the offer, my little cavaliere."

"I can lie about my age."

"We'll have no lying around here. Besides, you must stay in school."

"I can do both, work and go to school. School's easy. Please, Mama."

"That's very gallant of you," his mother responded with a smile, stroking his thick black hair, "but I could never allow that. You must give your best to school and what's left over must go to music. No, the only solution is for me to go to work."

So Adriana took a job with the Aetna Insurance Company in Hartford. She had always had a good head for math. With the experience of keeping the accounts for her husband's clothing store and a high score on the company's math test, she was made an actuarial assistant at a salary of $12,000 a year, enough to support herself and her three remaining children modestly in 1962. They had lost their home along with the clothing store and moved into a two-family house with the owners living above them. Every workday morning Adriana took a bus into downtown Hartford from her suburban town, then waited at a little depot station for another bus to take her along Farmington Avenue to Aetna's Head Office, an imposing brick building with a neoclassical facade staring across the avenue at Saint Joseph's Cathedral, a modern-looking edifice of white granite. At first,

Adriana would spend part of her lunch hour praying in this cathedral but its soaring columns and vast vaulted ceiling made her uncomfortable—it was too much like the cavernous office where she worked from 8:30 to 4:30 every day of the week. "I feel unimportant here too," she thought. "How can I feel close to God in a place like this?" And she stopped going. She spent her day at a small desk in an office of three hundred souls, making computations on her cash-register-sized Gestetner adding machine and entering figures in the narrow columns on long sheets of lined pale green paper. A bell would ring at 11:45 precisely for the lunch break and the three hundred people would instantly stop working, rise up en masse, file out into the hallway and herd down the stairs to the cafeteria. Another bell would sound at 12:45 to signal the resumption of work, and then at exactly 4:30 the final bell of the day would go off and the herd of people would move with somewhat more enthusiasm out into the hallway where they would join another herd of people and together stampede down the stairs and pour out into the streets. This deadening process was repeated day in, day out, five days a week.

II.

Adriana had lost almost all of her handsome furniture purchased in the first six months of her marriage and diligently, painstakingly paid for over the next four years, but one item she could not sell and fought hard to keep in the new apartment was her baby grand piano, a black beauty gleaming like a thousand nights of happiness. She had always been fiercely determined that one of her children would learn to play well enough to have a professional career, the career that she herself gave up when she married. Julian, her youngest, had shown the most promise.

At the age of five he had climbed up onto the bench, opened the cover, stared at the keys, and played the melody from a piece Adriana had been practicing. So the lessons began, with Adriana teaching him in her spare time, and as he grew older the lessons became longer and more intense.

All went well for a while. Julian made outstanding progress and Adriana's brother, Mario DeSalvo, who was an attorney, agreed to act as Julian's agent and business manager when his career was launched. A few good years passed, and then came the bankruptcy and her husband's disappearance, misfortunes that seemed to drop on her like boulders from the sky.

Yet Adriana was more unrelenting than ever about giving her youngest child a good start on what she knew would most likely be an arduous path towards success.

"He must go to a good conservatory, and the sooner the better," she told her brother, the lawyer.

"How about the Hartt School of Music?" asked Mario. "It's right here in Hartford, and I know some people there."

"No, no, no—I want him trained for a serious professional career, not something academic."

"You're wrong about that, 'Riana. They're very career-oriented at Hartt. Try to keep an open mind."

"Well, I'll look into it," said Adriana, closing the subject.

Not long after that came the news that her oldest son, the marine, was reported missing in action in Vietnam. Adriana showed tremendous strength during this ordeal. Her friends marveled at her fortitude in the face of yet another tragedy. "She is a tower of strength," some of her closest friends exclaimed to one another. "She is like Job," said a woman who had known her since middle school, and her listeners understood what was meant by that remark: Adriana deserved only the best from life but all she seemed to get was suffering and misfortune.

"Your mother has had a hard life," Adriana's brother told Julian one day. "And she is an amazing woman. Even as a young girl she was stronger than the rest of us children put together."

Julian, who was very earnest and sometimes trembled when he spoke said with a quiver in his voice, "I want to help her. I want to do something that will make up just a little for all the pain she's gone through."

"That's very noble, Julian. But it's not the kind of thing a son should ever impose on himself," the uncle replied.

"Why not?"

"Well, first of all your first obligation is to yourself, and secondly, you're not responsible for what your father did or anything else that's happened to your mother."

"I believe I am destined to help her," Julian fervently replied. "That's why I was put on this earth."

"Maybe so," said Mario. "Who am I to say? But I think it's choice rather than fate. You have the right to choose to devote your life to her if that's what you want. But you shouldn't neglect your own needs. You should enjoy yourself more."

"I do enjoy myself, Uncle. Don't think I don't. I have friends and we do things together."

"Like what?"

"Movies, baseball, fishing . . . when I have the time."

"When you're not playing piano, you mean."

Julian was silent, and Mario sensed he had said too much. He knew he had no right to interfere with his sister's plans.

It was early summer, and a few days later the uncle took his nephew to Charlestown, Rhode Island to prepare the family cottage for the new season. They drove down in Mario's red Alfa Romeo. Every minute of the two-hour ride was thrilling for Julian. "I love this car," he told his uncle. Mario smiled, remembering his own first love for cars.

The "cottage by the sea" was actually a plain three-bedroom ranch house purchased by Mario and his brothers in a suburban development near a lagoon. Julian loved it because it resonated with so many good memories of leisure and play with his cousins: long meals with some of his large extended family, his mother's laughter, his father's storytelling. Seeing it now, though, brought him only sad thoughts of his absent father and his brother lost in the jungles of Vietnam or a prisoner of the communists or worse. Aware of his sadness, Mario tried to distract him from these troubles by telling Julian he could have his first driving lesson. Every year a local couple came in to help get the house ready for summer. The winter tenants were college students who invariably left the house in disarray. When the clean-up work was underway, Uncle Mario took Julian out in the Alfa. On some of the open stretches by the beach Julian had his first driving lesson. His mastery of the gears came almost instantly—after half an hour he was able to shift through them with ease. "You're a natural talent!" Mario shouted as they cruised along in fourth. Julian was exhilarated.

"Uncle, I want to become one of the greatest of this century, one of the greatest concert pianists or one of the greatest racing drivers!!"

After they had pulled over and changed places, Julian asked his uncle if he believed in him.

Mario ran a palm over the top of his own moon-like head. "You've got talent and you've got the drive, but it takes more than that to make it in this world."

"You mean I have my mother's talent but I also have my father's bad luck. Is that what you're saying?"

"Not exactly. I don't think you can inherit bad luck," Mario answered, taking his driving glasses from the glove compartment.

"What about the Greeks and the Romans," said the young man astutely. "They believed that the sins of the father get passed on to the children. Do you believe that, Uncle?" The boy looked at him apprehensively.

"Gosh, no. Not for a minute do I believe in those ancient superstitions. There's no such thing as a family curse. Get that idea right out of your head, boy. It's poison. Your life is what you make it, and don't forget it."

Mario started the car and pulled out aggressively onto the road.

"I'm sorry. I didn't mean to upset you, Uncle."

"It's okay. I just get worked up when I hear stuff like that from young people. Especially gifted young people like you. Fatalism is an idea I've been fighting against all my life. I grew up with it."

"If you believe that a man is what he makes himself then how can you say I need luck to be a success? Isn't that what you're saying?"

"Julian, you can make your own luck by working hard. By being diligent, disciplined, and determined as hell. You succeed by choosing to succeed. By believing in yourself."

"I'll do whatever it takes to be the best. And that will make mama happy, won't it?"

"Perhaps. But what about Julian. Will it make you happy?"

Julian looked away. "My happiness doesn't matter. At least not yet. I need to make mama happy first."

His uncle's words came back to him as he was lying in bed that night, waiting for sleep. If what Uncle Mario said was true, then it must mean that his father did not believe in himself enough, and if he did not believe he was lucky, that he was meant to win, then he would always lose. Was it his father's fate to be unlucky? Was it his brother's fate to be lost in Vietnam?

Was it his fate to be a successful pianist and, if not, then what would it matter how much drive and determination he had? Julian puzzled over this, recalling what his mother had told him two years ago, that fate comes from God. Which was it? He fell asleep wondering.

III.

Soon school was over and the summer vacation began. Before the end of the school year, Julian had received notification of his acceptance as a contestant in the Goodwin Piano Competition for Young People. The competition was sponsored by the New York Philharmonic; the winner would be granted the opportunity to perform as a soloist with the famed orchestra—scholarship offers from the best colleges and conservatories would inevitably follow. This was the best news Adriana had had in some years—there was momentary rejoicing, and the intense preparations began. Julian's practice schedule was intensified—no time for the usual summer leisure activities, no time to take his friends on beach trips to the cottage in Charlestown or go with them and their fathers on camping and fishing weekends. He barely had time for his greatest passion, sandlot baseball, and his friends complained loudly and bitterly when he missed a game, for he was their strongest pitcher. "The piano must come first," was the philosophy his mother tried to drill into him. "When your friends are grown up they will not be playing baseball but you will still be playing the piano," she repeated day after day. "Besides, you cannot risk injuring your hands and fingers. That would be a tragic waste." Julian did not tell her everything, though. It wasn't baseball that threatened his career as much as two girls who came to watch him play. He didn't tell her that it wasn't music but these girls who occupied his last thoughts as he fell asleep on those warm summer nights. He didn't tell her because it didn't matter. He would not disobey her.

So his mother's will prevailed, and the piano came first. He looked upon it as his fate. "I will win first prize for you, Mama. Don't worry," Julian told her whenever she used one of her aphorisms or expressed any anxiety about his future.

Adriana was impressed by her son's confidence, but she replied, "You must work hard and pray to God every night, my little cavaliere. Without Him nothing is possible."

There was talk of little else that summer but the coming competition at Carnegie Hall. It seemed to Julian that his mother was focusing her entire existence on him and the competition, and he was resentful, wishing she had some outside interest, but then he realized it was her way of coping with her most recent misfortune, the disappearance of his brother, the marine. Yet winning seemed to matter much more to her than to him. He mentioned this to her and her response surprised him: "Of course winning would be wonderful, but it's not only that, it's the fact that my child, my precious one, will have his chance, his moment of glory in the sun. Don't you realize how much this means to me, after all the terrible things that have happened to us these last few years? Finally you and I could have what we both deserve—a moment to stand proud and tall in the eyes of the world." She wiped away the tears and her face brightened. "I've always known that fate had something good in store for us."

Julian smiled. "Where will we stay, Mama? In a hotel?"

"We will stay at one of the best hotels, the Waldorf. It's not exactly in our budget, but I've always wanted to stay there."

"How will we afford it, Mama?"

"Tush, nevermind about that. We will manage somehow."

"I don't think we should borrow any more money from Uncle Mario."

"Leave the details to me."

One day the following week Adriana came home early from work and was very disturbed to discover that Julian was not at the piano or anywhere else in the apartment. The twins could tell Adriana nothing, only that he had gone out. By the time Julian came home an hour later, Adriana was very agitated.

"Another five minutes and I would have come to that baseball diamond myself to fetch you. How many times have I told you that when those boys grow up—"

"I wasn't playing baseball, Mama," Julian interrupted.

"Then where were you? Did you go to the moon and back?"

"I was at the church, praying."

Adriana looked relieved. "Prayer alone is not enough, son. You must practice, practice, practice every day."

"I wasn't praying for myself. I was praying for brother and for father. I want God to bring them both home safely so they can be in the audience at Carnegie."

"May the good Lord answer those prayers. But as far as I'm concerned your father can stay wherever he is, and good riddance. Now you'll have to practice tonight to make up for the time."

Julian agreed readily, glad that his mother's questioning had ended; if she had continued she might have uncovered the truth: that he had been in the park with one of the girls who came to watch him play baseball. This was the first time he had told his mother an outright lie; the first time he had disobeyed her; his first experience of the stinging shame of guilt.

"Why are you home early today, Mama?" Julian asked with sudden fear.

"I had a medical appointment."

"Is something wrong?"

"No, it's nothing. Some tests, that's all."

"Tests for what?" the boy persisted in alarm.

"A woman, even a mother, must have some privacy," Adriana answered, and the subject was closed.

But the tests came back positive. Adriana's medical problem was diagnosed as ovarian cancer. Her condition was very grave. From her womb, the cancer could spread rapidly through her system. A hysterectomy was done at Hartford Hospital. The doctors were hopeful they had caught it in time, that all of the cancerous tissue had been removed. In a week, Adriana was home again, resting comfortably and supervising the household and Julian's practice schedule from the living room sofa.

"Your playing will make me well, my little cavaliere. And if not I will die in a state of bliss."

"Please don't talk that way, Mama," said Julian softly from the piano bench, his head lowered over the keyboard. "You're not going to die."

"I am going to do as God wishes. He will take me when He wants me. There is nothing I or you or anyone else can do about it." Adriana closed her eyes and put her head back. "Please begin with one of my favorites, won't you?"

Two of her favorite pieces were Debussy's Claire de Lune and Shubert's Impromptu #1 in F Minor. Julian played them repeatedly for her.

The weeks passed, and the music seemed to help her cope as much as the morphine which had to be administered in ever-increasing doses. At night, when the pain was worse, she would stay up listening to music. "I will stay up with you," said Julian. "Please go to bed, son," Adriana insisted. "I have the moon for company."

The day came when Julian could play no more. He held his

mother's frail body and wept uncontrollably. "I can't go on, Mama. I can't do it," he sobbed.

"There, there, my son. That's all right," Adriana whispered, stroking his hair. "There's always next year. Cosi sia. What will be will be."

"You must go back to the hospital, Adriana," Uncle Mario told her one night after dinner.

"Yes, Mother, you must," Julian agreed. "There must be something else they can do."

"No, no. The doctors have done everything they can possibly do. I will stay at home with my family."

She fell asleep on the couch, and Mario remained at her side, holding her hand. An hour later she opened her eyes and looked at him and then at the twins.

"You are still here," she said, and smiled. "My faithful brother. Where's my little cavaliere?"

"On the back porch. Do you want me to get him?"

"Let him be for now. Come closer, Mario." Mario leaned over, placing his ear next to her pale lips. "I have learned something important," she whispered. "The greatest accomplishment of my life. Do you know what it is?" Mario shook his head. Adriana closed her eyes and opened them again. "My children. I have such wonderful children. There is nothing greater in life. They have turned out so well." She smiled, and closed her eyes. Mario had seen joy in them for the very first time.

IV.

The next day Adriana said she felt a little stronger. When Julian heard this, he felt a surge of hope and went immediately to the church to pray. Kneeling in the pew, he murmured,

"Lord, please make her well again. Please, please, please, please, please make her well again, Lord. I am sorry I lied to her about praying for father and brother, although you know that is what I wish for every day and in my own way I guess I am praying for them so maybe it's not really a lie. She's had such a hard life, Lord, so many disappointments, and she's never lost faith in you. Never. Please, Lord. If you make her well I swear I will do something to help people. I will use this gift you have given me because I know it makes people happy when I play for them. I promise you . . . " and he continued in that vein for close to an hour.

That night he played again for Adriana, beginning with her favorite pieces, Claire de Lune and the Impromptu. She fell asleep listening to the music, and for the first time in weeks she passed the night comfortably.

The following day, Adriana was weaker and the nausea returned. Julian went back to the church to pray. That night, he played for her, but the pain came back again, only this time it was not quite so bad.

"How was your night?" Julian asked his mother anxiously at breakfast.

"Your mother is beginning to feel a little better, my little cavaliere. I am beginning to think that maybe my time has not come yet."

Adriana's doctor was amazed at her rapid improvement. He ran some tests and could not believe the results. Over the next few weeks her condition continued to get better. He had no medical explanation for what was happening—it seemed nothing short of miraculous.

"It is simply not my time yet, Doctor," Adriana told him.

Eventually, all traces of the lymphoma disappeared, and the doctors declared that her cancer had gone into remission. "Call it what you wish," was Adriana's standard reply, "but God has decided not to take me yet."

Overjoyed, Julian went to the church to give thanks and reiterate his promise to the Lord. "Now, Lord, please help my brother, please bring him home safely . . ." he prayed. That night his brother appeared to him in a dream. His face was radiant. "This place is filled with music and I am surrounded by angels. Our father is here too. Life passes like smoke but the Kingdom of God lasts forever. Live a good life and take care of our mother. Do not be sad, my little brother. I am happy now."

A week later Adriana received notification of her son's death and in another week his body was returned from Vietnam in a plain black casket draped with a flag. He was buried at Arlington National Cemetery with military honors. Julian did not tell anyone about his dream.

With her son lying dead before her, Adriana said, "The Lord has seen fit to take him now. I must not complain. I must accept this as his fate." But her emotions churned in anger.

"The poor fellow," said her brother Mario. "He should have gone to Canada. At least then he'd be alive."

Julian looked from his mother to his uncle. Could they both be right? Wouldn't his brother still be alive if he had made a different choice?

That night, in the hotel room in Washington, D.C., Adriana began to weep. Julian and his sisters tried to comfort her, but they could not. She wept inconsolably. "Why has God given me so much heartache? Why has my life been filled with so much sorrow? There's an old saying: 'God does not give you more pain than you can bear,' but this is too much suffering for one person to bear. How can I endure it? Lord, why have you given me more than I can take! What terrible sins have I committed?" Julian and the twins were frightened by their mother's lamenting and the intensity of her weeping. They had never seen her like this, so distraught and overwhelmed. The girls sat beside her on the bed and stroked her hair and arms while Julian stood by the window, crying and wishing his uncle would come back to help them. He called room service and ordered some tea. Then his uncle came in with a bottle of whiskey and his mother drank some and later had two cups of tea. She grew calm at last, said she felt better, and a little while later, worn out and exhausted, they all went to sleep.

The next day they returned somberly on the train to Hartford.

V.

Having seen her naked grief, Julian became even more determined to make his mother happy and he redoubled his efforts at the piano. He swore to do everything in his power to win first prize in the approaching Competition at Carnegie Hall.

At last the day arrived. Julian and his mother took the train to New York and checked into their hotel room at the Waldorf. After registering at Carnegie, they did some sightseeing, had an excellent dinner and were back at the hotel by seven. After watching a movie on television, Julian went to bed by ten. The next morning he was up at six o'clock. By eight, he was standing nervously in the wings of the famous Hall, awaiting his turn at the piano with a large group of very anxious, very talented ten, eleven and twelve-year olds. After a grueling ten-hour ordeal, the winners were finally announced. Julian had placed first in his age group. He was overjoyed. His eyes found his mother's eyes, and he saw pride in them, but only for a moment.

Later, when they were back in their hotel room, he asked her if she was proud of him.

"Yes, I am very proud of you. Your future looks very bright

now."

Julian thought he detected a note of jealousy but dismissed it. "We can use the money to pay off some of our debts."

"No, no, no—that money must be invested for your future. Uncle Mario will handle all that."

"You don't sound very happy, Mother."

"I am quietly rejoicing, my little cavaliere. It is not my way to dance around the room. Besides, one must accept what happens, either good or bad, with an even temper. I have learned it is better to take things in stride."

"I did it for you, Mother. I won first prize for you."

Adriana smiled and stroked his hair. "I know that. But it all turned out so well because God wanted it to. What God doesn't want will not happen."

Julian's disappointment became even stronger over the next few weeks. No matter how hard he tried, nothing seemed to please his mother as much as he hoped. She accepted the good things that happened as her entitlement and the bad things as her fate. It was exasperating. He decided to discuss this with Uncle Mario at their next "driving lesson."

The day of the "lesson" was overcast and before very long it started raining hard. Mario pulled the Alfa off the road into a picnic area and parked under some pine trees.

"What a summer it has been, Uncle. First mama's sickness, then brother's funeral . . . and we still don't know about father."

"Yes, all that is very sad. But you won the competition. That's fantastic! A dream come true! I'm very proud of you, and your mother is too, of course."

"She doesn't show it."

"That's not her way. She's never been very demonstrative about her feelings. I used to call her the Stoic."

"She chalks everything up to fate, and doesn't give me much

credit."

Mario shrugged. "What can you do with a woman like that?"

"Maybe dad left because he just couldn't deal with her anymore."

"Most likely that had something to do with it—we'll never know for sure. I guess you must miss him an awful lot."

"I guess."

"Too bad he didn't make it to Alex's funeral."

Julian wanted to say he knew his father was dead because of his dream, but he felt foolish. Suddenly, he was overcome by sadness. His throat constricted terribly. He fought the tears but they sprang from his eyes and ran down his cheeks.

"What's wrong, Julian?" Mario asked with heartfelt concern.

"Oh, Uncle, I'm so miserable most of the time. Nothing is working out the way it's supposed to." His anger flared up. "I've worked so freakin' hard and, well, what's the point—what the hell is the point! I just want to chuck everything and go away somewhere, and just do what I want for a change—play baseball, go fishing, whatever."

"Don't throw it all away. You've worked so hard. Just give it more time," said Mario. "You've got real talent, and with hard work and . . . well, you could be on top of the world someday."

"And luck. You were going to say luck, weren't you?"

"Everybody needs some luck."

"And I was born without any, like my father."

"Don't be so negative—you won the competition, didn't you? Maybe that's the turnaround—maybe your luck has just kicked in."

"You're just saying that to make me feel better."

"No, I really mean it. I wouldn't lie about a thing like that. Look, the rain's letting up. Want to take her for a spin?"

But Julian wanted to go home, and Mario started the engine

and pulled the car onto the road. The boy's eyes were filled with tears, and the anguish of a soul in torment was plainly visible on his face. Mario drove in silence; he felt powerless; there was nothing he could do to help his nephew, and that made him very uneasy.

That night, Julian had a marvelous dream. He heard music of profound beauty, a chorus of celestial voices, and saw a sunrise of gold, silver, gray and yellow over a gold-burnished sea. Out of the sky came a vision of a huge angel with flowing dark hair, a lovely white face and neck, long blue robe, and silver wings tipped with fire. The angel's eyes were large and dark and inexpressibly beautiful. Behind the towering angel were three tiny figures that grew larger as they approached until they were large enough for Julian to see their faces. Each figure carried a banner with a name emblazoned in gold letters but Julian would have recognized them: they were Johann Sebastian Bach, Wolfgang Amadeus Mozart and Antonio Vivaldi. The music swelled to a crescendo and then ceased. One by one, the figures climbed up on the angel, with Bach on her head and Mozart and Vivaldi on her shoulders. Taking turns, the composers spoke to Julian in quiet voices that sounded like oboes, clarinets and bassoons, saying: "You are an artist. You must create. It is the artist's job to create. You must not shirk that responsibility. It will not be easy. Being an artist never is, but it is the greatest calling that can come to a human being. Take heart. You must put aside all other plans. You must quell your fears and anxieties. Have faith in yourself. Trust your talent. Work hard and in due time the rewards will come. This is your destiny . . . " The music began again, and the angel with the three figures started to recede back over the ocean until they all faded away in the clouds.

Julian woke up. He was frightened and elated, and sad, too,

that the strange dream had ended. Had he really dreamed of a huge angel surrounded by the figures of Bach, Mozart and Vivaldi? What did it mean? And why wasn't Beethoven among them? Was music truly his calling? Was he born to be a composer? A hundred questions whirled through his mind. It was still dark but he was too agitated to go back to sleep. Dressing quickly, he went outside and climbed the Japanese maple tree in the backyard. He sat there thinking. As the sun came up, Julian was filled with inner peace and he thanked God for sending him a vision. He was certain now that music was his destiny and that he was an artist. The decision was made for him. It was simple. Everything fell beautifully into place. This was his moment of great joy.

VI.

The years passed. Julian finished high school and went on to the Hartt School of Music in West Hartford on a full scholarship. After college, he started giving concerts with orchestras around New England. Audiences went wild over his virtuosity, his style, his charisma. A telephone call came from Leonard Bernstein himself, inviting Julian to perform at Tanglewood with the New York Philharmonic. His performance was a triumph; his luck had indeed changed, and his career had blossomed. But he had not yet composed a single note of music.

One evening after dinner in their new home in West Hartford, Julian asked his mother if she were happy. She replied in the affirmative and looked down at the table, but Julian had seen the old sadness in her eyes and the lines of pain form around her mouth. She looked older now: her hair was half gray and more lines were etched in her face, but to Julian she was still very beautiful.

"There's a full moon tonight. We should go out on the terrace. I have always loved the moon," said his mother.

Watching her face and the familiar movements of her head as she spoke, her subtle gestures, Julian realized that there was something about his mother he would never understand—the deep sorrow that never went away. The sadness and tragic sorrow at the core of her being made her an enigma to him. She was a very profound mystery he would never solve. She meant more to him than any other person on the face of the earth and yet he could not understand her. How ironic! The thought that in the ten years since she had almost died he still had come no closer to understanding her and that someday she would go to her grave without his understanding her any more than he did at this moment was a horrible sadness for him. Julian looked at her large beautiful eyes and realized how much they meant to him, how important they had been to him ever since he was an infant gazing up into them from his cradle. His mother's eyes, full of love, longing, hope and sadness but never joyful, sometimes filling him up and sometimes as distant as the moon. His mother's eyes would always hold that look of deep sorrow that he could never take away no matter how many prizes he won, how many concerts he gave, or how much money he earned. He wanted so desperately for her spirit to be joyful and her heart to be filled with peace, and he knew in this moment that it was never to be and there was nothing he could do about it. He must accept her as she was, and he knew he must go on loving her as much as he could.

"Mother, I must tell you about a dream I had many years ago. Just before we went to Washington for Alex's funeral he appeared to me in a dream and told me he was in a place where angels were singing."

She smiled. "Yes, I am sure he's in heaven."

"And, Mother, he told me father is there with him." He watched in surprise as his mother began to cry. "Why are you crying, Mother?"

It was a moment before she could speak. "I don't know. Life can be so terribly, terribly disappointing. I didn't want my family to end up like this."

"I will always be here for you, Mother." But the words sounded hollow in Julian's ears. He had recently begun to long for his independence with a strong passion.

"No, Julian, you must follow your own path now. That is the way it should be."

Julian saw the truth of this in his mother's eyes. Someday very soon he would have to leave, but he would always love her. He recalled his dream of the three composers. He looked again at his mother and saw his destiny in her eyes.

This Man Moses ✦

WHEN I HEARD that Moses and the children of Israel had been delivered by his God from out of the land of Pharaoh, I took my daughter his wife and her sons who had returned unto me and we went out into the wilderness to meet him. Moses and his people, of whom there were multitudes, were encamped at Rephidem near Horeb, at a place called the mount of God, and we went out there unto them.

When Moses learned of my presence he came out to receive me, and I said, I thy father-in-law Jethro am come unto thee, and thy wife, Zipporah, and her two sons with her: Gershom, whom you named thus because you were a stranger in a strange land, and Eliezer, so named by you because the God of your father delivered you from the sword of Pharaoh. And Moses kissed and embraced me and did other obeisance but did not greet his wife and his two sons who stood close by.

Now this man Moses remained alike in his appearance and actions unto the man who had lived with me and my daughters

and tended the sheep and become as one of my own sons. I
marveled to look upon him for he was still the modest man who
had left me to do the work of God. He asked of my welfare and
that of my family and I inquired of his and of his people, whom
I said seemed well. Then he looked upon his wife and his sons,
and I saw that he knew them. He spoke with Miriam his sister
and bid her care for them and treat them well. All the people
who were there, even the elders, saw and heard the way Moses
spoke of them who were his wife and his own flesh and blood.

Alone in his tent we sat upon rugs laid out on the hard earth
and I asked how they had fared in the wilderness and what it
was that they had eaten to sustain them since they had departed
from Egypt three months ago. Moses said that their food had
fallen from heaven and was something called manna. He had
some there, and I ate it. It was a whitish pellet of resinous gum
resembling the bulbs that drop from the tamarisk, and it tasted
like a wafer made with honey. Moses told me that this manna
fell at night and cooled upon the ground and had to be picked
up in the early morning before the sun rose. He said, too, that
quail had dropped from above, and that his people had eaten of
their flesh to satisfy their hunger. Moreover he told me that the
people had murmured against him, complaining of their
privations. Would to God we had died by the hand of the Lord
in the land of Egypt, when we sat by the fleshpots, and when we
did eat bread to the full, they said to me. The whole
congregation of the children of Israel murmured against me,
Moses said, and then the Lord said unto me, Behold, I will rain
bread from heaven for you, and at even ye shall eat flesh; and it
was as God had spoken to me: in the evening the quails came
down and covered the camp, and in the morning the manna lay
amidst the hoar frost on the ground.

God is good, I replied and said to Moses that he must know

the land well now that he had crossed it a third time.

I learned much that first and second time, Moses replied, when I left you and returned to my people in Egypt. Yes, I learned much in those days, for when I came to you in Midian I still behaved like an Egyptian even as I dressed as one; but it was through you that I came to Joseph, Jacob, and Abraham; it was with you that I learned of the man Moses and of his God.

I knew of these things already, for he had told me of his first encounter with God at the sacred place on the mountain when God's voice had come to him out of a burning bush that was not consumed, and still I marveled at them, as did he. Indeed, I saw now that although his physical appearance remained the same, this man Moses had changed much, for there was a light in him that shone from his face in rays. Tell me of the things that you have seen and done, I asked him, since you went out from my house.

He did tell me then such stories as I have never thought possible: how the Hebrews had come out of Egypt and what their God had done for them. Against Pharaoh, whose heart was hardened against them, God did send a series of plagues, ten in number, within the space of a year. First, the waters of the Nile were turned to blood and then spat forth frogs of such limitless number that they did creep even into Pharaoh's bedchamber, but still Pharaoh's heart was as stone and he would not let Moses and his people go. Next came a murrain among the Egyptians' cattle, then calamitous hail, a plague of locusts and a terrible darkness—all these things fell hard upon the Egyptians. Among the people, Moses said, the Lord had given us favor but still Pharaoh's heart was turned against us, and the Lord said to me: About midnight will I go into the midst of Egypt, and all the firstborn in the land of Egypt shall die. And he commanded me to tell the children of Israel to spread the blood of a lamb upon their doorposts that the Lord would know their houses and pass over them. All this came to pass, said Moses, and the lamentation was very great, for the Lord smote all the firstborn in the land of Egypt. The next day, Pharaoh called for me and for Aaron and told us to rise up and go forth from out of the land of Egypt. And we took our journey from Succoth and encamped at Etham, and the Lord went before us by day in a pillar of cloud and by night in a pillar of fire. Thus he showed us the way to follow.

Here he paused to listen to some voices outside the tent. A quarrel had broken out, and rising, Moses went out and spoke to the men who were in disagreement, and their quarrel stopped. Seated near me again, he took up the rod that he had from the time he had been with me and extended it, saying, the Lord's power is in this. It is not mine but the power of the Lord, he repeated. And I was struck by the brightness of the rays that streamed from his face. With this staff, he said, was Pharaoh's army destroyed.

I looked at him, and he saw that I did not understand.

This is the staff given to me by God, he continued, and when we came to the Red Sea I lifted it, and the Lord parted the waters; and when we had passed through, I went up to a high place and beheld that the armies of Pharaoh came after us with their horses and their chariots, and so I held this rod aloft, and the Lord closed the waters over them, and they died.

He was reluctant to say more, and so I did not press him further as I knew that speaking was always difficult for him, and he had already spoken at length, a thing rare for him, and something I took as an honor to my person. Yet then I perceived that he needed to say more, and so I waited for him to go on.

I would not have you think, Father, Moses said, that I believe it is my power that accomplishes these miracles, for I know that it is the Lord's. And this is how I know. He lifted his hand and stared at it a moment as though he had something quite particular to say to me about it; but then he fell silent and said no more whatsoever.

I rejoiced for all the goodness which the Lord had done to Israel, and I said, Blessed be the Lord, who hath delivered you out of the hand of the Egyptians, and out of the hand of Pharaoh, who hath delivered the people from under the hand of the Egyptians. At last the power of Egypt is weakening! I exclaimed. Let us have a covenant meal; I wish to make an offering to the Lord. And Moses too rejoiced and said it would be done.

While the preparations for the meal were taking place, I inquired of my daughter Zipporah and her sons and was told the way to Miriam's tent. I entered, and was surprised to find them alone, for Miriam was not with them, and I asked how they were being treated.

O, Father, did you see how he looked at me, as if I were some unwanted thing that had come back to him? Please, Father, take me away with you. I should never have come here.

You are his wife, I replied. I am sure he will send for you now that our greeting is concluded.

We have talked, Gershom, Eliezer, and I, and we want to return with you to Midian. Tell your grandfather, my sons, that this is what you wish to do.

Gershom and Eliezer answered out of fear for their mother, but there was no such wish in their eyes. It was plain to me that their desire was to know their father, for this man Moses was clearly a source of fascination to them, and they hungered to be with him.

My daughter, I began, we have traveled far and you are weary.

You must rest. In a few days all will seem different to you.

No, Father, it is only now that I can see clearly. In a few days, when I have rested and have grown comfortable, I will not have so plain a view of him.

And what is it you see? I see a man who cares much for the welfare of others.

That is true, but it is not enough for a wife. He has always cared much for others. When I first met him, dressed as he was, he was not like an Egyptian. He stood up to the shepherds who bullied us and drew water for our flock. I have not forgotten that. She drew a step closer to me. In the wilderness not far from here on our way to Egypt, a strange thing happened concerning the Lord and Moses, something I can never speak of, but it made Moses need me more. And when I returned to you with my sons it was to wait for him while he performed the duties the Lord had asked of him, and I knew that my being with him then would not be wise. But now he does not need me, and if I stay then I will grow weaker until it will not matter to me that he doesn't need me. And I will become a thing of pity and of scorn. I do not belong here. These people will never accept me. Even now, Miriam—

At that moment, Miriam entered, and I could see immediately the haughtiness in her manner. She flashed her eyes at Zipporah, who looked down with shame at her impropriety. Miriam then said to me, My brother Moses awaits you with Aaron and the elders. As I left, I gave Zipporah a glance that was meant to be reassuring. There was a pain in my heart, for I knew that between those two women, Zipporah and Miriam, there would never be peace.

Moses and the elders were assembled for the meal when I arrived. Aaron too was there, standing beside his brother. Praised be Yahweh, said Moses.

Yahweh? Was this Most High God of Israel also the god of my people? I wondered. Had he left Mount Sinai of Midian to go before these tribes?

The commencement of the Covenant meal, for so it was called, was quite awkward. We stood before Moses's tent, and the elders expected him to conduct the service. But Moses did not seem inclined to do so, and he turned to me and asked me to begin, but I declined, deferring to him; I suggested furthermore that we sacrifice one of the cattle I had brought with me from Midian; as this was acceptable to all, I had the most favored one fetched up for us.

While we were making the burnt offering, I proclaimed as I had earlier that day when Moses and I were alone in his tent, Blessed be the Lord, who hath delivered you out of the hand of the Egyptians, and out of the hand of Pharaoh, who hath delivered the people from under the hand of the Egyptians. And then I continued, Now I know that Yahweh is greater than all gods: for in the thing wherein they dealt proudly he was above them. The elders seemed greatly astonished by my use of the name Yahweh and they regarded me with keen interest.

I have been a priest of a nomadic people for most of my life, and always my God was the mountain and fire god who spoke to Moses from the holy place on Mount Sinai of Midian. He was always there with us, but now it seemed that he had left us and attached himself to these children of Israel and had kept his promise to them. What more would he do for them, this Yahweh; what glories and blessings would he bestow on them? I wondered, too, *why* he had chosen them in particular—what special qualities did they possess and what would he do now that they had murmured against Moses? I had many questions which might never be answered.

Do you believe, asked one of the elders, a man with large

hands and rounded shoulders, that Yahweh is also the god of the Midianites?

I have come to recognize, I replied, that your God is the truest form of my own God.

That may be so, returned the elder, but he is the one who is present with us now, who upholds and protects us. I have seen with my own eyes, dim though they may be, how he parted the sea and brought death to the Egyptians. The God of the Israelites is the Lord of all nature, and what he has done for us he has done for no one else.

Tell us, Moses, asked another of the elders, is Yahweh also the God of the Midianites? If that be so, has he not left them and attached himself to us?

There was fear in the voice of the next elder who spoke. Does this mean that he may abandon us here in the wilderness and return to the mountain in Midian?

It is true that he will do whatever he wishes, Aaron said, and as he has spoken to Moses so have I told it unto you. The people have complained of their privations since leaving Egypt; they have seen the hand of God at work and yet their faith is weak. The Lord has helped Moses draw them out of slavery, he has promised them new life, and still they grumble that they would rather be slaves. They would have the sting of the taskmaster's whip instead of the caress of God. And in crying out against Moses they cry out against the Lord. By their murmurings they show themselves unworthy. It may provoke his anger and he may smite them. If the Lord wishes, he will destroy the children of Israel and return to the Midianites.

Do you think he will do this, Moses? queried the elder with the large hands.

He will do as he wishes, Moses replied. The children of Israel are a stiff-necked people, and this does not please him. More than this I cannot tell you except, it is not I who rule over you but the Lord.

Our feast ended, and Moses accompanied me to my tent. I was about to ask him if he would speak to Zipporah and his sons when he cried out, With the help of the Lord, I delivered the children of Israel from slavery to freedom, from a land of death and death worshippers unto a new life, and yet they dare to murmur against me—and so against God.

Be not too harsh with them, Moses, I counseled, For they have only recently come out of slavery and are afraid. The wilderness is a strange and frightening place for them; neither are they accustomed to living in it, as we are. Furthermore, beware that the discontent of the people become not a burden to you, for I fear that you take their unhappiness too much to heart.

It is I and no other who has led them here. They look to me for help.

It is Yahweh who brought them here, and it is he who will lead them out.

True, Father, but now they are angry, and it is I whom they wish to stone. This rod is heavy in my hands. I asked not to be made leader of his people. I told him I have not the tongue to speak the words they need to hear. They will not believe me, I answered God when he spoke to me in Midian; they will not listen when I tell them you have appeared to me. Father, I said many foolish things to the Lord because I did not feel strong enough to lead these people. And so, God's anger was kindled against me for my reluctance to accept his command.

Does not your worthiness appease him? I asked Moses the prophet.

I do not know that I am worthy, for I cannot prevent the murmuring and when I go to God and tell him of their needs and ask that they might be satisfied, I fear that he will say to me: Why canst thou not teach the people to obey me and keep my laws? Why canst thou not silence their murmurings? Perhaps it is too much to ask of them. I do not know. I have always been a free man, but they have only been slaves. Perhaps that is all they can ever be.

The following day I rose with the sun, and when I went out I came upon the prophet Moses surrounded by many of his people. And all day long he sat amidst them so that neither I nor Aaron his brother nor Miriam his sister nor any of the elders could approach him and speak with him. Later that morning, and after lunch, and in the afternoon I returned to him, but always was he surrounded by his people so that I could not get near him.

That afternoon my daughter came to me and said, Father, where is this man Moses and why does he not come to me and my sons?

I have seen Moses the Prophet surrounded by his people since just after the sun rose, I told her, and I went there to speak with him in the morning, after lunch, and late in the afternoon, but always the people congregated before his tent and I could not get near him.

What will I do? cried Zipporah in distress. This man who is my husband will not come to me, and does not even acknowledge his own two sons. His sister Miriam is cruel to me, but how can it be otherwise considering the way her brother is treating me? I must speak with him, Father.

My daughter, you cannot speak with him today, I replied.

Then you must speak with him for me. If you cannot then you must take me away with you. I do not wish to be the wife of a prophet. He has his God. He does not need me.

That evening I went to Moses and found him alone in his

tent. His face was pale and the light that emanated from it was now very dim. What is this thing that you were doing with the people today? I came to you in the morning and at lunch and late in the afternoon, but I could not get close to you. Why do you sit thus alone while all of your people crowd around you from when the sun comes up until the time it goes down?

Because the people come to me to inquire of God. They bring me any matter that they have to be decided, and I judge between one and another. Thus do I teach them the statutes and the laws of God.

This thing is not good, I said. You will surely wear away if you continue to do this, both you and your people. This is too great a task for you to perform alone.

The Lord will say to me, Why didst thou not teach the people to obey me and keep my laws? He will grow angry, and he will say, For not doing this thou will not enter the Promised Land. Yet I fear that I will not be able to do this, and I will never see the land that was promised to Abraham's seed. The children of Israel are a stiff-necked people, and they grow more and more unmanageable. The tribes are stubborn and jealous of each other, and they are losing respect for the institution of the elders. We fought a battle with the Amalekites who attacked us here in Rephidem. Joshua chose his men and went out to fight with them. But, Father, the Israelites have no knowledge of battle, neither do they know how to organize themselves for such an undertaking, and if it had not been for this staff they would have been destroyed, for I did stand upon the top of a hill with the staff of God in my hand and what I saw was a scattered and disorganized people.

Harken unto my voice, I said, and I will give thee counsel.

I then told Moses that the Midianites were familiar with caravans and military exploits and that there was a system of

organization which he must borrow from them. It was essential
that he do this, I told him, for two reasons: the first being his
own health, for this burden he had taken upon himself would
surely kill him, and the second was the preservation of his
people in the wilderness, for without some form of organization
they would all perish. No one knows more about survival in the
wilderness than a nomad, I said, and there are no better nomads
than the Kenites. Moreover I said that by adopting this system
he could yet fulfill his promise to Yahweh to teach his people
the Lord's ordinances and laws.

But will justice be done to those who are in disagreement?
Moses asked me, and I told him that it was he who must ensure
that justice be done. Furthermore I said that he would be able to
endure and that all his people would go to their Promised Land
in peace.

So Moses chose able men out of all Israel and made them
heads over the people, rulers of thousands, rulers of hundreds,
rulers of fifties, and rulers of tens. And they judged the people
at all seasons: the hard cases they brought unto Moses the
Prophet, but every small matter they judged themselves.

And so at last I left him, and my daughter Zipporah, and her
two sons, and all the children of Israel, and I returned unto my
home in Midian. But before I departed I gave Moses directions
how he should go through the wilderness, and I appointed
certain Kenites to be among those who traveled with him. And I
forbade Zipporah to leave him, for I was convinced that this
man Moses would need her, and, besides, I wanted my daughter
to be among those who were so well-favored by God.

Blues for the Common People ⚜

THE LITTLE GUY walked into the bar with a woman who was twice his size. A few heads turned. The regulars who saw them in the mirror corkscrewed around on their stools to take a good look. A fat man winked at the bartender and jerked his bulbous skull in their direction.

They made a tawdry pair. The man was wearing a powder blue summer suit and an open-necked shirt which revealed gold chains against a hairless chest; his black hair was slicked over in an attempt to cover his scalp. The woman was obviously a hooker.

The little guy and the hooker sat down at a table right out in the midst of the more conservative customers. It was not much of a bar, but the management didn't go for this sort of thing. There were dark corners for this type of clientele.

"Guess they didn't see us," the little man said after they had waited for a waitress to take their order. "I better get the drinks myself."

He approached the bar and drew himself up.

The bartender was frowning. "What'll it be, bud."

"Gimme a Jack Daniels straight up and a banana daiquiri."

Sullenly, the bartender made the drinks.

"Five even."

The little guy peeled off a five and a one, and took the drinks over to the table where his date was waiting with a cigarette for company. She was somewhere between virginity and the grave. Her hair was very fine and naturally kinky, and her heavily mascara-ed chocolate brown eyes were not the dead globes of jelly or the hard-as-glass peepers endemic to her trade. Everything else about her was typical of the tribe, though, from her tight-white pants, red high-heeled shoes and pink halter-top to the overall swollen quality of her figure. There were deep brown lines in the palms of her hands and a jaded look on her face. Her lips were painted a shade of purple and pinched to one side as if she were sucking the inside of her mouth between her teeth.

"I said a strawberry daiquiri. This one's banana." Her voice was raw and shrill.

"I'm sorry, honey. I'll get you a strawberry next time," the little man said calmly.

"But I don't like bananas. What am I, a monkey or something?"

"Awright. Jeez, don't get worked up about it. I'll get you a strawberry."

The bartender scowled as the little man's head and shoulders approached him again so soon. "What's the problem, bud."

"She told me strawberry. I ordered banana."

The bartender's black eyes shot quickly along the bar. He wanted to make sure he had an audience for this. "Yeah. I heard." He stood leaning back against the shelves of liquor, seemingly determined to make it as difficult as possible for the little guy.

"So, could ya make a strawberry."

"Well," said the bartender in the same laconic style, "I'd have to charge you."

"I figured." The little man smiled and shrugged. "Whatever Lola wants . . . " he quoted.

"That's right," the fat man piped, unable to contain himself any longer. "Whatever Lola wants. She ain't no monkey."

No one else laughed. The bartender made the drink and the little guy paid him, gave him another dollar tip, and returned to his table.

"Say, what's the idea of calling me Lola? I don't like that."

"It was just a joke, honey."

"I don't care. I don't like that kind of thing."

"Don't get sore. I didn't mean nothing."

"I don't like that fat guy. Who the hell does he think he is. You let him make fun of me."

"You gotta consider the source. He ain't nothing. He's just a blob with a big mouth."

"Well, I don't like it here. This ain't my territory."

"You gotta break out of the rut once in a while. Try new places."

"Why should I? I like the usual places."

"You gotta see the way other people live. Driving the cab, I get to talk to all kinds, and, you know, I try to see the other guy's point of view."

"Everybody's the same."

"How the heck can you say that?"

" 'Cause it's true. You can't tell me any different. Guys want to stick it, and gals want to sell it. That's about the size of it."

"Aw, that's too simple. It don't explain everything."

"Oh, no? It's what makes the world go around. You take it

from me. Mrs. So-and-so with her marriage certificate ain't no different from me. She sells her sweet tocus to the man who keeps her."

"That's an old one. I've heard that before."

"The only difference between her and me is volume. If you can keep selling to the same guy over and over then you've got a good thing going."

"Women don't need to rely on a guy for a livelihood no more. They can earn their own way now."

"You telling me? I've been doing it since I was seventeen."

"Awright, awright. Jeez, can't you cut me any slack? I came out to have a good time tonight."

"Don't let me stop you."

"Don't get sore. I didn't mean nothing."

They finished their drinks and the little guy stood up to get another round.

"Sit down," said the hooker.

The little man was back in his chair. "What's the matter, honey? You want to go?"

"No, I want another drink. But they're going to come to us this time."

"I don't know. I wouldn't count on it. I know this place, and—"

"You know, I just figured something out," the hooker continued. "You brought me here to show me off, didn't you? You brought me here 'cause you want to let these bums know that you're somebody. Ain't I right?"

The little fellow remained silent.

"Well, I know I'm right, even if you won't admit it. And listen, I believe in giving a guy his money's worth. We'll show these dudes that you and me are somebody. We'll show these honky dudes that you, my little white man, have got the stuff to take care of a big black mama like me."

"Jeez, I—"

"Shut up and just go along with it. Waitress. You come over here, the man wants to order."

"What the heck's the matter with you? Want to get us thrown out of here?"

"What're you scared of? You want to stay a little man all your life?"

"I am a little man. There ain't nothing I can do about it."

"If that's the way you feel . . . " said the hooker with one hand on her purse.

The little man flashed her an angry look. "Sit down. The waitress is coming over." The creases on either side of his square jaw became deeper and longer, matching the carved grooves in the table. His fingers drummed on the dark varnished wood where initials, names, and cryptic messages recorded the graffiti of the passage of time.

The hooker's face was a glossy plum; there was a gloating look in her eyes. The little man caught a whiff of her, and he thought he could smell Africa. She was like a big, dark, mysterious continent to him.

The waitress was a middle-aged crone, round-shouldered, stout, and mean-looking. Her voice was a thin screech. "Now you listen here. I don't go for this kind of—"

"I don't care what you go for," the hooker cut in. "The man wants a drink. Ain't you a waitress? Ain't it your job to take his order?"

"You can't talk to me that way!"

"I just did."

"Why, you ain't nothing but a—"

"Paying customer," the little man said sharply. "We're paying customers and we're entitled to some service."

"I oughta slap her face." said the waitress sourly.

"Try it, honey."

"We're paying customers," the little man repeated as though he had discovered a charm in that phrase. "That's just what we are. We'll take a Jack Daniels straight up and a strawberry daiquiri."

The waitress eyed the folded bills in the little man's hand. "I don't have to take that kind of talk from nobody," she grumbled as she jotted down the order and left.

"Dried up old bitch," the hooker hissed. "I'll knock her teeth out. What're you laughing at?"

"I ain't laughing at nothing."

"Crap. You're laughing at me. Calling me Lola. I don't go for that kind of thing. Uh-uh."

"I like you. You're all right, you know that?"

"Hah. Look at you. You feelin' bigger already."

The waitress brought the drinks over and collected for them. The little man gave her a two dollar tip which she did not acknowledge.

"That's right. You feelin' bigger and bigger. Ain't you?"

"You're all right," the little man said again.

They sipped their drinks in silence for a time. The hooker fidgeted, angled her big body in the captain's chair, swung her long legs in the aisle and crossed them.

"What's wrong, honey? You want to go?"

"I don't want to stay here all night."

"We'll have one more round and then we'll go."

"Look at your face. My, my, but you are pleased with yourself. It's always money that does it for you white dudes. Spending money makes you feel like a man, don't it."

"I'm enjoying myself. Don't spoil it."

"Shoot, having money don't make you a man."

"Don't you think I know that?"

They lapsed into silence again. The deep creases returned to the little man's face. He was pondering something of great importance to him.

"Jeez, look at all these names carved into the table. Who the hell were all these people?"

"It don't matter."

"I guess it don't. But, still, it makes you think."

"It makes me sick," said the hooker as she lit up another cigarette. "Nobody cares who these people are. It's like the stuff you see on the subway in New York. It's obscene. Nobody cares. Why do they bother?"

"What makes people do it?"

The hooker blew a plume of smoke. "Damned if I know," she spat out disdainfully. "Who knows what makes people do the crazy things they do. If I knew the answers I'd be a millionaire. What makes you what you are? Can you tell me that?"

The little man was caressing the table top. His mood had turned reflective. "I could-a made something of myself."

"Don't start that kind of talk. It depresses me."

"But look at me. I'm a loser. Don't I look like a loser?"

The hooker did not reply. "Listen, you must have a secret fantasy. Tell me about that."

"What the heck are you talking about?"

"A secret fantasy. You know, the person you'd be if you could change yourself into whatever you wanted. Tell me about that. Who would you be if you could be anybody at all?"

The little man thought for a moment. "I'd be Elvis." he said decisively.

"You mean Elvis Presley? The King himself, the King of rock and roll?" the hooker said, laughing with great beauty.

"Why, don't that beat all! He was some dude. You picked yourself a winner there."

"Now I'll tell you something else. I used to do Elvis impersonations."

The hooker's large eyes grew larger. "No! You're kidding me."

"I'm telling you the truth. I used to have an act, a real professional act. I used to be able to sound just like him. If you heard me you couldn't of told the difference."

"Is that right? My, my. Why'd'ja give it up?"

The little man shrugged. "Couldn't afford the costumes. Other guys were doing it too, and I needed a whole lot of expensive things to compete, costumes, lighting, a good back-up band. Things just didn't go my way. I needed a manager, and—aw, heck I just got too old for it."

"That's the bitch about life, ain't it? It's better to die than to get old."

"That depends on the shape you're in."

"It's different for a man."

The little man looked at her without speaking.

"I want another drink," said the hooker.

Stretching around, the little man tried to get the attention of the waitress.

"The old bitch is ignoring us again."

The little man stood up. "I'm going to the bar," he declared.

The bartender looked at him once with animosity and then kept his face averted. "I'm sorry. I can't serve you."

"We're paying customers," said the little man. "And I'm—"

"I don't care who you are. Nobody talks to my waitresses the way she done. You treat my people with respect or you don't get served."

"That's right," the fat man chimed in. "This ain't the jungle down here."

The little man put his money away. He was about to leave, automatically turn and go away, but then he opened his mouth and spoke words he had had no intention of speaking.

"Your waitress insulted my friend. Who does she think *she* is?"

The waitress was glaring at him from her station at the end of the bar. She bristled when she heard this, and her sour face turned even more sour.

"Now, look, bud—"

"No, *you* look," the little man declared, his voice swelling with anger. "Just because I'm a little guy and she's a hooker doesn't give you the right to push us around. We're paying customers like anybody else. And what's more, we're citizens of this country, too, with the same rights as you and everybody else. I drive a hack for a living—you ain't no better than me. You think you're better than us?" He swiveled his head to look at the waitress, who turned away in disgust, then swept his glance up and down the bar. "Is there anybody here who thinks he's better than me?"

No one spoke. The bar became completely silent. The fat man was studying the little guy with an amused grin. The bartender folded his arms and leaned back. Everyone else avoided looking at him. The little guy turned around and stared at the other customers seated at the tables. No one met his challenge except for the hooker, who smiled with admiration.

"You get in my cab, I take you where you want to go, regardless of who you are," he went on. "I don't ask questions. This is America, ain't it? Sure we got our problems, but this is still the place where everybody's got their rights."

There was a long silence. Everyone looked down, stared at their hands, peered into their glasses; no one could meet the little guy's gaze.

Finally, the bartender spoke up. "Go sit down. I'll send a waitress over."

The hooker was beaming when the little man returned to his table.

"You were marvellous," she said with a big smile.

"Sometimes you just got to stand up to people," the little man replied.

"It looked like you planned the whole thing."

"Nope. It caught me by surprise. Just before I opened my mouth I thought, what would Elvis have done?"

A younger waitress came over to serve them. The little man told her they were all set and had to be running along. Then the little guy and the hooker who was twice his size walked out of the bar together.

Also available from Lorenzo Press

THE DISCOVERY OF LUMINOUS BEING
a novel by Anthony Maulucci

The word is getting around

"A highly lyrical, bittersweet, romantic story."
—Bill Brownstein, Montreal journalist

"Excellent work . . . The story has the quality of a Picasso line drawing . . . I enthusiastically recommend this novel."
—Herb Gerjuoy, writing in *The Red Fox Review*

"Brave fiction, bristling with the authentic ring of autobiography, the pain and glimpses of joy inherent in real life."
—Elisavietta Ritchie, Toronto author and poet

"Maulucci is enormously gifted."
—Don Gastwirth, San Diego attorney

"An engrossing, well-crafted tale . . . Some very fine writing that increases with every page. Maulucci superbly captures the charms of Montreal."
—the *Norwich Bulletin,* Norwich, Connecticut

Order from your local bookstore or online from amazon.com